**'You look ... come in a ... myself clea...**

Sara sensed she was blushing as she handed Michaelis a couple of clean towels. 'I tend to get myself into nurse mode whenever I've been working on an emergency case,' she said briskly. 'My only concern is that you don't catch cold from being in the water for so long.'

Michaelis leaned forward and put his finger under her chin. 'You're very kind to look after me like this. I'm pretty tough, but thanks for your concern.'

She held her breath. For one delicious moment she thought Michaelis was going to kiss her.

Briefly she allowed herself to remain absolutely still, revelling in the closeness of this fascinating man. His finger under her chin must be receiving an electric current of smouldering passion from her. She felt sure Michaelis must feel it. But looking up into his eyes she saw only sadness. Here was a bruised, hurt man whose emotions couldn't respond.

**Dear Reader**

I've been in love with the Greek islands for many years, especially the island of Ceres (not its real name). It's so relaxing you want to stay there for ever, wandering in the hills along deserted paths before going down to one of the spectacularly beautiful bays where you can swim in the crystal-clear waters of the Mediterranean.

I decided that Ceres was the perfect setting for my Greek Island Hospital mini-series. I happened to be lazing on a beach out there in the hot sun one day—as you do!—when I started to get the idea for a story about three sisters, the daughters of a famous surgeon, all of them medically qualified, who go out to live on Ceres and work in the hospital. There would be a wonderful sense of community in the hospital, just as there is among the delightful, friendly people on this idyllic island. So I started writing…

**Greek Island Hospital** was born, and DR MICHAELIS'S SECRET, the story of Sara, the youngest sister, a staff nurse, who falls in love with the ruggedly handsome but elusive Dr Michaelis, is the first book in the trilogy.

Look out for the stories of Sara's two sisters, nursing sister Chloe and the enigmatic doctor Francesca, both in Mills & Boon® Medical Romance™ later in the year.

I hope you'll enjoy reading the three stories as much as I've enjoyed writing them. Being back on the island of Ceres with Sara, Chloe and Francesca has given me hours of pleasure. I hope you'll feel the same when you put the final book down.

Happy reading

*Margaret Barker*

*All the characters in this book have no existence outside the imagination of the author, and have no relation whatsoever to anyone bearing the same name or names. They are not even distantly inspired by any individual known or unknown to the author, and all the incidents are pure invention.*



*First published in Great Britain 2003*
*Harlequin Mills & Boon Limited,*
*Eton House, 18-24 Paradise Road, Richmond, Surrey TW9 1SR*



ISBN 0 263 83427 1

*Set in Times Roman 10½ on 12 pt.*
*03-0203-45988*

*Printed and bound in Spain*
*by Litografia Rosés, S.A., Barcelona*

# DR MICHAELIS'S SECRET

BY

MARGARET BARKER

MILLS & BOON®

# CHAPTER ONE

SARA gazed out across the sparkling blue, blissfully peaceful sun-kissed water of Nymborio Bay. It was difficult to believe that this time last week she'd been firmly entrenched in the hurly-burly life of Accident and Emergency at Moortown General Hospital. And now here she was, starting her new life on her favourite Greek island.

Ceres… Just the very sound of the island's name was enough to give her goose pimples on the back of her neck. Ceres was a Greek goddess, wasn't she? Somewhere at the back of Sara's mind she remembered hearing a fascinating story when she was a child about Ceres and her daughter Proserpine. Sara had loved all those bedtime stories her mother had told to her and her sisters, and she remembered vividly being fascinated when she found out they were all going to stay on a Greek island called Ceres.

All those wonderful holidays the family had enjoyed here when she was a child! The people so friendly, the scenery so magnificent, the Mediterranean food so wonderfully exotic…

She stretched out and wiggled her toes on the sun lounger, smiling to herself as she realised that she'd been thinking in travel agent speak. It was almost as if she wanted to convince herself she'd done the right thing when she'd come out here to join her parents and one of her sisters.

Sara's mother, Pam, had raved so much about how

wonderful it was now that she and Sara's father, retired surgeon Anthony Metcalfe, were actually living on the island that it had been difficult for Sara to withstand the idea of coming out to join them.

'Not wishing you were back in dear old Moortown, are you, Sara?'

Her sister Chloe's voice broke into her thoughts.

Sara grinned, swinging her legs over the side of the sun lounger to place her bare feet on the ancient, uneven paving stones of the wide terrace overlooking the bay. A large seagull was swooping down towards the water where a fish, dicing with death, was recklessly rippling the surface. The silver scales of the fish shone in the sunlight as the gull lifted it out of the water in its beak and soared up above the bay.

'What do you think, Chloe? Do I look as if I'm pining for the freezing cold March weather back in England!'

Chloe ran a hand through her hair as she stood looking down at her younger sister. 'I'm really glad I came out to join Mum and Dad last summer. The twins love it here; their Greek is coming on in leaps and bounds now they've started school and they have lots of little Greek friends to play with.'

Sara watched Chloe as she moved over to sit on the chunky stone wall that ran around the terrace. Tall, slim, with long blonde hair, Chloe looked tanned, healthy and carefree, and much younger than her twenty-eight years. The Greek lifestyle had certainly taken away the careworn look she'd had since the tragic death of her husband six years ago.

Sara stood up and padded barefoot across the stone paving of the terrace to sit beside her sister on the wall. Looking down at the stone jetty that jutted out into the water, she could see her two little dark-haired nieces stripping off their clothes.

Sara smiled as she pointed down at the children. 'Are Rachel and Samantha actually going to swim today?'

Chloe pushed her hair away from her blue eyes, settling it firmly behind her ears. 'They talked me into letting them swim this afternoon. I don't think they realise that even though the sunshine is a lot warmer than in England it's still only March. Most Greeks won't go into the water until August.'

'Look at Mum!' Sara watched her mother removing her sweater and trousers to reveal a black swimsuit on her small, slender figure. 'The cold water isn't going to put her off!'

Their petite blonde mother turned her face upwards, shielding her eyes from the sun. 'Why don't you two come down and join us?'

'No, thanks,' Chloe said. 'I'm helping to get everything ready for tonight.'

'Looks like it!' her mother said, as she ran along the jetty and dived off the end.

'You'd never think Mum was fifty-two, would you?' Chloe said. 'Somebody asked me the other day if she was my sister.'

'I hope you told Mum about it.'

Chloe smiled. 'Of course I did. She said it made her day! But you've got to hand it to her. Mum does work hard at keeping fit and trim.'

Anthony Metcalfe, their father, remained seated on the jetty, fully clothed in jeans and sweater. Ten years older than his wife, he was still managing to remain fit and athletic. He was tall, but over the years he'd adopted a slight stoop. Probably from all those operations he'd performed, Sara always thought when she looked at him nowadays. His hair was still brown, like her own, but flecked with silver at the front and sides—which gave him a distinguished look, in Sara's opinion.

'I'm on lifeguard duty,' he called up to his daughters.

Shrieks of laughter almost drowned his voice as the seven-year-old twins paddled in the shallow water under the watchful eye of their grandfather. Manolis, the man who did the heavy work in the house and garden, and ferried the family around in the boat, was also down at the water's edge.

'Manolis is an expert swimmer,' Chloe told her sister. 'I don't need to worry about the twins when he's around. Dad looks happy, doesn't he? I think taking early retirement and buying this place was the best thing he could have done at his age. He's still young enough to enjoy life without that hectic, demanding work that was sapping away all his strength.'

'I don't think it was so much the actual operations he performed as everything else he was expected to do,' Sara said. 'Lectures, conferences, seminars, newspaper articles, television appearances. That was what used to exhaust him. He never wanted to be a famous, sought-after surgeon, did he?'

Chloe smiled. 'I remember Dad always used to shy away from the lifestyle that surrounded his status, didn't he? He's at his happiest wearing an old fisherman's jersey, out there in the middle of the bay on his boat, fishing.'

Sara flung back her head so that the sun would shine full on her face. 'It's so beautiful out here. No wonder we all love it! What's it like working in the hospital?'

Chloe stood up. 'I love that too. Come and help me in the kitchen and I'll tell you all about it. You've got a couple of days to settle in before you start work.'

Down in the kitchen, it transpired that Maria, Manolis's wife, who came in several days a week to work as housekeeper-cum-mother's help, had got everything under control. Maria explained that she'd already prepared the homemade taramasalata, olives and other small delicacies which she was going to serve with the pre-dinner drinks on the terrace. When they were all seated at the table she would serve the fish she'd prepared with fresh herbs gathered from the hillside. The fish was barbouni, she told them—red mullet—fresh from the sea that morning. Manolis was going to grill several of them on the barbecue outside the kitchen door.

'I don't think Maria wants us to help,' Sara said as she and Chloe retreated from the kitchen.

Chloe smiled. 'Maria prides herself on her self-sufficiency. She's arranged for two of her married daughters to come round from Ceres town to help her serve this evening.'

'So who's been invited?' Sara asked as she went into the sitting room and sank down into one of the squashy armchairs. She looked around admiringly at the warm ambience her mother had created since moving in to the house.

This was one room that seemed typically English in décor. Pam Metcalfe had arranged for most of the furniture to be shipped out from England. There were a couple of huge sofas covered in a dark red fabric—

very dramatic, like her mother, Sara thought. The squashy armchairs, by contrast, were covered in a cream-coloured cotton which matched the curtains, tied back beside the windows.

The antique oak coffee table in the middle of the room held the books and magazines that they all intended to read but rarely got around to. At the end of the table was an ancient sewing box that had belonged to their maternal grandmother. Sara knew that this was one of her mother's most treasured possessions. They had never known their grandmother, who had died before they were born. This precious memento had always held pride of place in their home, even though Sara had never seen her mother pick up a sewing needle in her life! Pam Metcalfe was no skilled needlewoman.

Looking around the room now, Sara realised that only the stunning view from the long, wide windows leading out on to the terrace reminded them that they were on a Greek island.

'Mum wants it to be a welcome dinner to introduce you to some of the staff you'll be working with at the hospital. Some of them you've already met, when we were out here on holiday. There's Michaelis, for example…remember Michaelis, who came over to England for that surgery course Dad agreed to organise at Moortown General? Mum invited him home to dinner and you got a fit of the giggles.'

Sara felt the colour rushing to her face. Even at twenty-seven she hadn't outgrown the annoying habit of blushing, and doubted she ever would now.

'Well, I was only sixteen, and Michaelis's English had me in stitches! I shudder to think how rude I must have seemed, but whenever you, me and Francesca were together on those formal kind of occasions, where we'd been told to behave ourselves, there was always something that would start us off giggling. Have you heard from Francesca recently?' Sara added, trying to change the subject from that memorable evening eleven years ago.

Chloe shook her head. 'One phone call since Christmas. Our big sister has a busy life in London. Has Francesca been in touch with you?'

'I usually phone her every couple of weeks. Sometimes she's out and I leave a message. She usually rings back, but I get the impression she's rushing around trying to forget that boyfriend of hers. Ever since they split last summer Francesca seems to have been working long hours at the hospital or madly socialising.'

'She'll wear herself out. Mum would like her to come out and join us here. They never have enough doctors on the island. They're constantly having to expand the medical services at the hospital and she'd be sure to find a job there. I mean, don't you think it would be a good idea for her to get away from London and make a fresh start?'

Sara looked thoughtful. 'It would be fantastic to have all of us together again,' she said carefully. She knew that sophisticated Francesca wouldn't take kindly to having her future mapped out by her sisters. 'But I'm not sure Francesca would settle down here after her hectic London lifestyle.'

Chloe sat down on the sofa, curling her long legs beneath her. 'I know that Francesca will do what she wants to do, as she always has done, but sometimes she needs us to point her in the right direction. She may be the eldest but that doesn't mean to say she's the wisest.'

Sara remained silent, wishing that Chloe wouldn't always try to sort out everybody's problems. Chloe was so kind-hearted. But she had enough problems of her own without playing mother hen to everybody else.

Chloe uncurled her legs and sat up straight. 'Anyway, to return to this evening. You'll be surprised when you meet Michaelis again. His English is near perfect now, apart from a charming Greek accent. It was his first time in England, you know, when he came for dinner, and I think he was struggling a bit. But he managed to tell us he'd been married a few months before and he described how beautiful his wife was.'

'Yes, I remember now.'

How could she ever forget! Sara gazed out of the window across the blue waters of the bay, trying to calm the emotions that were stirring inside her. A donkey was trotting along the path that zigzagged its way up the hillside. What a slow and steady pace! Everything was so peaceful here. It was just what she needed after the last few hectic weeks—finishing her work at the hospital, saying goodbye to everybody, packing up her flat, buying new clothes…

'Didn't you used to have a crush on him, Sara?'

'Me! Michaelis wouldn't have looked at me with you and Francesca around—and anyway, he was married!'

Chloe seemed amused. 'But when we were teenagers it was all very innocent. We just used to look at men and decide who we fancied, didn't we? And I definitely remember you told me that—'

'OK, OK!' Sara laughed. 'I was only sixteen. It was eleven years ago. But, yes, I remember I thought he was rather dishy.'

'Rather dishy! You said afterwards—'

'Yes, I admit I thought he was rather gorgeous, in that swarthy, muscular, Mediterranean, husky-voiced—' Sara broke off. 'I'm sounding like a teenager again, aren't I?'

She closed her eyes and leaned back against the cushions of her chair. 'I think I did have a crush on him at the beginning of dinner, but after Mum put him next to me and he made rude remarks about my spots I went off him. Anyway, he was far too old for me at twenty-six. Tell me about his wife. Is she…?'

'His wife died just a few months after he came back to Ceres. I heard about it when we came out for our holiday that summer. But that was the year you went to France on an exchange visit so you missed all the news.'

Sara frowned. 'How sad! She can't have been very old. Why did she…?'

Loud voices coming up the stairs announced that the twins were back from the water.

Chloe jumped up. 'I really don't know.'

'Mummy, Mummy!' Rachel and Samantha came bounding in, wrapped in towels. 'We saw a big fish.'

'It was that big,' Rachel said, stretching her arms.

'No, it wasn't. It was this big!' Samantha's arms were as wide as she could possibly stretch them.

Chloe laughed. 'I'm sure it was enormous. Come on, let's get you two into the bathroom.'

Sara jumped to her feet. 'I'll help you, Chloe.'

Two wet little hands clasped Sara's on either side of her as the twins propelled her out through the door.

* * *

'The calm before the storm,' Sara said as she sipped her glass of orange juice on the terrace.

After helping Chloe with the twins, she'd squeezed some oranges into a large jug in the kitchen. She'd found that the ouzo and retsina consumed at these gatherings on Ceres went straight to her head, and she was getting well prepared with something she knew she could drink throughout the entire evening—interspersed with the odd glass of wine, just to appear sociable.

'I wonder who'll be the first to arrive this evening.'

'It's the calm after the storm as well,' Chloe said, smiling. 'I thought we'd never get the twins into bed. Thanks for helping me with them tonight. They always enjoy it when you read them a story at bedtime.'

'I love being with the girls. It reminds me of the fun we had when we were kids.'

'You mean before we grew up and—' Chloe broke off as her voice choked.

Sara reached across and squeezed her sister's hand affectionately. 'It's been so hard for you, Sis.'

'It's much easier now,' Chloe said. 'And being part of a big supportive family has been a great help... Look, there's a car coming along the road...there across the bay beyond the trees. I think it's Michaelis's Land Rover...yes, it is. He drives to the hospital in it and I've seen it parked outside.'

Sara stood up and glanced around the terrace at the cushions placed on the chairs, the dishes of nuts and olives on the little wooden tables. For some unknown reason she hadn't wanted Michaelis to be their first arrival. She'd wanted the place to be humming and buzzing with people so that she could merge in with the crowd and wouldn't have to engage herself in conversation with him.

She glanced up at the hillside, where the last rays of the setting sun were streaming down to turn the waters of the bay into a fiery pink and orange cauldron. It was thoughtful of her mother to arrange this party in her honour, but suddenly she felt nervous about meeting up with her new colleagues. Especially Michaelis, whose Land Rover was fast approaching along the gravel road.

Sara went to the edge of the terrace and looked over the wall. Down below, at the water's edge, a couple of walkers in shorts and tee shirts were putting down their rucksacks and taking off their boots. The woman put a toe in the water and squealed in a mixture of delight and shock as the cold water made contact with her feet.

'Go on, Jonathan. Get your feet in this water. It's so soothing. Oh, it's fantastic!'

Sara smiled. Everywhere on this island people knew how to enjoy themselves. This couple had probably been walking all day over the hills and now were winding down ready for the joys of an evening's relaxation.

The Land Rover had almost reached the house. Now it was grinding to a halt. Michaelis was getting out. She drew in her breath. She'd forgotten how handsome he was. Over the last eleven years she'd merely glimpsed him occasionally in Ceres town during her brief visits.

She'd recognised him, but he'd never given any indication that he recognised her. The first time this had happened had been about three years after Michaelis had been over to England. It had been at the height of the tourist season, she remembered. She'd been with a group of friends, but she'd hoped for some sign of recognition from him. A nineteen-year-old could get very hurt by a snub like that!

'Come on, Sara, stop daydreaming! Let's go and meet Michaelis.'

'You go, Chloe. I'll wait here.'

'Please yourself…' Chloe was halfway down the stone steps that led to the courtyard.

All too soon Sara could hear Chloe's footsteps returning on the staircase.

'And here's Sara…you remember Sara, don't you, Michaelis? You sat next to her at the dinner table at our house when you were over in England.'

The tall, handsome Greek smiled, revealing strong white teeth. 'This can't be little Sara! She was…'

'Go on, say it!' Sara challenged him in a bantering tone. 'I'm still little, but then I was fat, spotty…'

'No, no, no!' Michaelis protested, making wide, sweeping, gallant gestures with his hands as if to emphasise his point. 'What I am trying to say is that the young Sara was…well, she was…how do you say it? She was a teenager with all the problems of growing up. Whereas here we have a beautiful, sophisticated, svelte…'

Sara laughed. Michaelis was even more dishy than she remembered!

'OK, I forgive you for calling me spotty.'

'I'm sure I didn't call you spotty, Sara. I was struggling with my English, I remember. Perhaps I—'

'What will you have to drink, Michaelis?' Chloe intervened tactfully.

'I'd like a glass of water to start with, Chloe. I came straight from the hospital. I'm very thirsty and alcohol will only increase my thirst. Now, where was I?' Michaelis looked down at Sara with dark soulful eyes.

Sara smiled up at him. For someone so vibrant and effervescent there was a deep sadness in those eyes that hadn't been there when she'd seen him all those years ago. The eyes belied the happy, positive manner he'd adopted. He was putting on an act. She was sure of it.

'You were trying to explain why you told me I shouldn't eat chocolate. It was bad for my spots and it would make me fatter.'

'Did I say that, Sara? I'm sorry. I was a very young, inexperienced doctor and, as I've said before, my English wasn't good, so whatever I tried to say came out in a strange way that I hadn't intended. What I meant was that you were destined to turn into a beautiful young woman.'

Sara laughed. 'Flattery will get you everywhere!'

She decided that Michaelis was fun to be with, but it seemed as if there was a protective shell around him. His words came out easily, in a flirtatious manner that didn't quite ring true. She was sure that if she began to reciprocate his flattering remarks he would move away. It was as if he'd perfected the art of socialising without giving out anything of himself.

More people had arrived and were coming up the stairs. Chloe introduced Sara to Andonis, a charming Greek doctor who was accompanied by a small, dark haired, friendly-looking staff nurse.

'Call me Katie.' She smiled. 'Everybody does except my Greek grandmother, who insists on my full name, Katerina. My Mum's Australian; my Dad's

Greek. I was born in Australia and lived there until last year.'

'So you've got relatives here on Ceres?' Sara asked, holding out a dish of olives towards Katie.

Katie chewed on an olive and reached for another one. 'You bet! Everywhere I go I keep meeting another long-lost relative. It's great! I love it here.'

'Everybody loves our island,' Michaelis said in his deep, sexy, resonant voice.

He swept his hand out towards the bay as if to emphasise his point. 'Just look at those mad tourists enjoying their swim out there. If they were in England now—' Michaelis broke off, frowning. 'They're going much too far out. Unless they're very good swimmers—which I very much doubt from all that splashing around—the woman definitely needs help. I'm going down there…'

'You're right, Michaelis,' Andonis said, putting down his glass. 'I'll come with you.'

'I'll get Manolis,' Sara said quickly, running down the steps behind the men. 'He's an expert swimmer. Manolis! Manolis!'

Seconds later they were all at the waterside—Andonis, Michaelis, Sara and Manolis. Michaelis, barefoot but fully clothed, dived off the end of the jetty, quickly followed by Manolis.

Sara realised that as she stared out across the water she was holding her two hands fingers upwards, under her chin, in a prayerful stance.

'Please let them be safe,' she whispered under her breath. 'Let them all be safe,' she added, as she watched Michaelis cutting through the water in a punishingly fast crawl.

Tonight was the first time she'd spoken to this man

for eleven years, but already he'd made a profound impact on her. The emotions of her teenage years had come churning back. The instant attraction she'd felt towards him all those years ago had been heightened unbelievably.

Out there in the deep waters of the bay Sara could see the rescue operation beginning. From where she was standing it looked now as if the woman had disappeared below the surface. She held her breath as she watched Manolis dive down in an obvious attempt to find her. Michaelis was supporting the exhausted man in a classic lifesaving position.

Her spirits lifted as she saw Manolis emerging from the water with the unconscious figure of the woman. Both Michaelis and Manolis were now heading back to shore. She breathed a sigh of relief, but knew they were by no means safe yet. And as Manolis bore his burden nearer to the shore Sara could see the woman looked completely lifeless.

Maria had come out of the house, carrying towels. As soon as Michaelis reached the shore with the man Sara wrapped towels around them.

'I'm OK,' the man spluttered as he sank down on to the shingly shore. 'It's Jane you've got to look after… Jane! She was tired. I was trying to hold her above the water, but…agh…Jane! Jane…'

The man moaned in horror as he saw the deadly pallid colour of his motionless wife.

'Take the man inside, Andonis,' Michaelis instructed as he lifted the lifeless body of the woman from Manolis.

Sara noticed that Michaelis was out of breath. 'I'll start resuscitation, Michaelis, while you get your breath back,' she said, quickly kneeling down beside their patient.

Leaning across the woman, she felt for a pulse. There wasn't one. Nor was there any movement in the chest. She turned her patient on to her side and a gush of foam-like froth emptied itself on to the shore. Placing her hand on the woman's throat, she put her fingers in her mouth as she attempted to clear an airway. The woman's face was congested and livid in colour. Sara bent down and closed the nostrils by pinching them with her thumb and index finger before sealing her lips over her patient's mouth and blowing gently into her lungs, two slow, full breaths with a pause in between.

She found herself willing her patient to breathe, but she still seemed completely lifeless.

Michaelis put a hand on Sara's shoulder. 'There's still no pulse. I'll begin chest compressions. We'll work in tandem. Give two breaths, Sara, and I'll follow with fifteen compressions.'

They repeated this sequence four times, checking the woman's pulse again. Still no sign of life. Sara took a deep breath and bent her head over the patient's mouth once more.

After several more sequences Michaelis detected a faint pulse. He called out excitedly, 'There's a pulse...oh, thank God!'

At the same moment Sara noticed a slight movement in the woman's chest.

'She's breathing, Michaelis!'

Sara, kneeling on the hard shore, raised her eyes and looked across their patient's body to Michaelis. It was a magical moment. The first time they'd worked together. And what had seemed as if it might turn into a tragedy had turned into a success.

Michaelis leaned across and took hold of Sara's hand. 'Well done!'

There was a slight spluttering sound from the woman. Michaelis turned her on to her side as more water gushed from her mouth and then, miraculously, her eyes fluttered open.

'Where's Jonathan? Where am I?'

'You're quite safe now, Jane,' Sara said soothingly. 'We'll take you inside to see Jonathan.'

It seemed strange to resume the party after the near drowning emergency as if nothing untoward had taken place. But then, as Sara's father reminded everybody, most of their party were medical professionals and they'd got used to switching from working to leisure mode.

The emergency ambulance which Anthony had called had dashed round from the hospital, causing some of the cars of late-arriving guests to pull over into passing points along the narrow road. By the time the two casualties had been handed over into the capable hands of the paramedics and loaded into the ambulance Anthony and Pam Metcalfe had got the party going again.

Only Sara and Michaelis were still missing from the groups of people gathered in the sitting room and moving around on the terrace. After handing over her patients to the care of the paramedics, Sara, concerned that Michaelis was soaked to the skin and beginning to shiver, had taken him up to the guest room and instructed him to strip off his wet clothes and take a shower.

Standing outside the guest bathroom, he looked down at her and raised one eyebrow. 'You look as if you intend to come in and make sure I scrub myself clean, Staff Nurse.'

Sara sensed she was blushing as she handed Michaelis a couple of clean towels.

'I tend to get myself into nurse mode whenever I've been working on an emergency case,' she said briskly. 'I'd forgotten for the moment that you're the doctor. My only concern is that you don't catch cold from being in that water for so long. I've put a clean pair of Dad's jeans and a shirt and sweater in the bathroom. The jeans will probably be a bit short on you. If you'd prefer to give the party a miss and go home, we—'

She broke off, unnerved by the amused smile on Michaelis's face. 'Sara, I wouldn't miss your welcome party for anything. You're very kind to look after me like this.

He leaned forward and put his finger under her chin, tilting her face so that she was looking up at him. 'I'm pretty tough, but thanks for your concern.'

She held her breath. For one delicious moment she'd thought Michaelis was going to kiss her. There was always a certain amount of elation at the successful outcome of a medical emergency, and emotions were apt to become heightened. She'd noticed it often before. But she'd never before worked with someone who had such a disturbing effect on her.

Briefly she allowed herself to remain absolutely still, revelling in the closeness of this fascinating man. His finger under her chin must be receiving an electric current of smouldering passion from her. She felt sure Michaelis must feel it. But, looking up into his eyes, she saw only sadness. Here was a bruised, hurt man whose emotions couldn't respond.

But would she want him to respond so soon? Of course not, she told herself firmly. Whatever transpired between them in the future she would have to go slowly. In her considered medical opinion, this man hadn't yet recovered from losing his wife—and maybe he never would. And anyway, maybe he wouldn't want her. A heart-throb man like this could have anyone he wanted.

She turned away, annoyed at herself for fantasising so much. 'I'm going down to join the party,' she said quickly. 'Come down when you're ready, Michaelis.'

She heard the sound of the bathroom door closing as she ran down the stairs. With her wickedly imaginative inner eye she had a momentary vision of Michaelis stripping off. Those fantastic rippling muscles, that attractive dark tanned skin, the way his eyes seemed to pierce inside her very soul…

She shivered as she reached the terrace, where the guests were chattering noisily. The candles on the tables had been lit, the overhead lights had been dimmed and out over the sea the dark, velvety sky was illuminated by the moon. It was the perfect setting for a party.

'Come over here, Sara,' her father called. 'I was just telling our guests that it's a good thing we're most of us in the medical profession, otherwise we would have had to cancel the party tonight. Once we knew that our two patients were out of danger your mother and I made the decision that we wouldn't change anything.'

Anthony Metcalfe put his arm around Sara's shoulder and drew her towards a man who was standing by himself, looking out across the bay.

'Sara, I'd like you to meet one of our non-medical guests. Stavros, this is my daughter, Sara.'

The stocky Greek man gave an almost imperceptible bow and smiled. 'I am very happy to meet you, Sara,' he said in a courteous tone. 'Your father tells me you are interested in music.'

'Well, I…'

'Sara has a degree in music,' her father put in quickly. 'From the time she was small she expressed a wish to become a concert pianist, and she's very good.'

'So what made you change careers and become a nurse?' Stavros asked.

Sara hesitated. 'Oh, it's a long story. Basically, when I left college I decided that I wasn't going to make it as a concert pianist and so I decided to do something more useful, like the rest of the family.'

She wasn't going to go into the trauma of that turbulent year when she'd changed direction. She was used to people asking her why she'd left the music profession, and usually her shortened version satisfied them. Even her father hadn't asked too many questions, but then he'd always been supportive of whatever she'd decided to do.

'But don't you miss it?' Stavros asked. 'I don't think I could ever give up music.'

'Stavros is a musician,' Anthony said, smiling, as he moved away to speak to another guest.

So this was why her father had introduced her and then left her to get on with it! Sara cleared her throat. 'I don't miss music because I always make a point of joining in music-making wherever I happen to be.

And I intend to have my piano shipped out as soon as I can arrange it.'

Stavros frowned. 'You'll have great problems with getting a piano here. The transportation on our ferries is fraught with difficulty. And then there's the problem of tuning when you actually get it here. The hot dry summers and cold damp winters have a bad effect on pianos. But I wish you luck. I'm one of the few people on the island with a piano. You're welcome to come and practise if you'd like to.'

'That's very kind of you.'

Sara was touched by the gesture of friendship, but there was something about this intense man that she wasn't sure of. Despite the Greek charm, he seemed almost nervous of being with so many people from the medical profession when he himself was an outsider.

'Excuse me.' Chloe came up behind Sara. 'So glad you're catching up with the musical life on Ceres. Stavros organises our annual music festival.' Chloe smiled at Stavros. 'You'll have to get Sara involved. Actually, at the moment I need to take Sara away from you, so that she can circulate and be introduced to some of the medical colleagues she'll be working with at the hospital.'

Sara smiled at Stavros as Chloe led her away. A useful contact to have if she was to get her music life back into focus, and the music festival would be a good start.

She found herself desperately trying to remember all the names and say something appropriate to each of the guests she was introduced to, but invariably found her mind was somewhere up there in the guest bathroom. Michaelis would be drying himself by now. He would be…

And there he was!

She drew in her breath as Michaelis appeared at the door, looking as if he'd spent the entire day resting. Even wearing the borrowed ill-fitting jeans and shirt he looked extremely well turned out, and his broad, trademark smile was perfectly in place. Sara watched as every eye turned to watch his entrance.

What a show-stopper! What a heart-throb!

She wondered if she was the only person in the whole gathering who'd worked out that it was all a façade. Every single movement of that fantastic body was designed to show the world that he was over the trauma in his life. Designed to show everybody that he was functioning normally. When in reality…

'Now that we're all here,' Pam Metcalfe said, raising her voice above the noise of the conversation, 'let's have dinner. If you'd like to follow me down to the dining room….'

# CHAPTER TWO

SARA looked around the dining room as she led the way with some of their guests. The everyday round family table had been relegated to a corner of the vast, high-ceilinged room which occupied most of the ground floor. In order to seat all twenty guests, Sara's father, helped by Manolis, had resurrected the large, rarely used wooden table that he'd bought with the house.

'What a perfectly wonderful table!' Katie exclaimed. 'However did you get such a huge piece of furniture out here?'

Pam smiled. 'It came with the house. The previous owner had it made here in the dining room, for some grand occasion, and it's actually too big to be removed through the doors or the windows. Usually it stands in sections, leaning against the wall behind that large screen, and we use the smaller round table over there.'

Sara moved around the table helping guests to find their places. Her mother always insisted on making a seating plan. Sara remembered the times when she and her sisters had tried to rebel by saying it was an outdated idea. But as they'd grown older they'd come to agree with Pam that lots of people liked to have a designated place as soon as they reached the table. There would be plenty of time to wander around and chat to everybody when they reached the coffee stage and were feeling more mellow and socially secure.

'I always put a lot of thought into where I place my guests,' Pam Metcalfe would tell her daughters whenever they aired their doubts. 'I usually know where everybody would like to sit.'

Looking now at the names of the two men who'd been placed on either side of her, Sara had mixed feelings. Michaelis was to be on her right, Stavros on her left. This was going to be one interesting evening! She would have to work on making Stavros lighten up a bit. But Michaelis would be stimulating in more ways than one.

Sara stood behind her chair as she watched Michaelis strolling in, chatting to a couple of the nurses she'd been introduced to earlier. He looked perfectly at ease. Maybe she was wrong about him. Perhaps it was something in her own make-up that induced a certain melancholy in him.

Stavros was coming over. Sara smiled, and was rewarded with a smile in return. Yes, he didn't look quite so intense when he smiled. He was thawing out. She'd noticed the way some of the guests had approached him to chat about the forthcoming music festival. It wasn't until August, but apparently there was a great deal of interest in the plans Stavros was making.

Stavros nodded his approval as he picked up his place name. 'I'm pleased to be sitting next to you, Sara. We can carry on our conversation about music.'

He moved sideways to take hold of Sara's chair and hold it out for her. As she sat down Sara looked up to see Michaelis standing beside her, his hands clenching and unclenching as he looked across at Stavros. She held her breath. From the deeply hostile expression on Michaelis's face she was expecting some verbal abuse to be forthcoming at the very least, but he maintained a stony silence. Turning away and ignoring the musician completely, Michaelis took his place on the other side of Sara.

This was such a strange situation. Neither man had acknowledged the other and Sara sensed a brooding atmosphere between them that she could have cut with a knife. As one of the co-hostesses with her mother she felt it her duty to try to lighten the tension.

She glanced from one to the other. 'I expect you've met each other before?'

Michaelis nodded. 'That's correct,' he said, in a steely voice.

Stavros turned to look at Sara. 'On a small island everybody knows everybody else.'

'And what everybody does,' Michaelis added quietly.

Sara shivered. There had been a certain ominous timbre to Michaelis's voice when he spoke, and the tension was patently obvious. But what could have caused this hostility? Any number of things, she supposed, and she wasn't even going to speculate. Here, in her own home, she was meant to keep the peace and make sure everyone enjoyed themselves.

She looked across the room towards the long serving table where Manolis was cutting up the fish he'd barbecued. Maria and her two daughters, resplendent in black dresses with white frilly aprons, were carrying the plates of garnished fish to the table and distributing them amongst the guests. The party was going well. There was a good level of conversation going on. Everyone seemed to be enjoying themselves. Even Stavros was deep in earnest conversation with the lady doctor on his right hand side.

'Your father told me you studied music at college before you did your nursing training,' Michaelis said to Sara in a conversational tone.

'Yes. I decided it would be better to join a useful profession like the rest of my family.'

Michaelis smiled at her. 'You sound as if you've had to explain that to people quite often.'

Sara smiled. 'You could say that.'

'I remember you played the piano for us when I came to dinner at your house,' he said, softly. 'I very much enjoyed your playing. It was something by Debussy, I remember.'

'*Clair de Lune*?'

Michaelis nodded. 'Yes, that's the one. I've got it on disc.'

'I'm surprised you remember me playing.'

Michaelis shrugged. 'I thought it was a very moving performance for such a young girl. That's all I do remember about the evening.'

'Except my spots!'

Michaelis laughed. 'Can we forget about your spots now?'

He leaned sideways, so that his face was very close to hers as he pretended to examine the skin on her face. 'Yes, in my considered medical opinion, the patient has been cured!'

As he leaned closer Sara could smell the freshness of the soap from his shower, and she sensed an attractive, indefinable masculine aura that appealed too much to her. But all too soon Michaelis ended his mock medical examination.

'I'll happily forget about my spots for ever!'

Sara put down her knife and fork and leaned back against her chair. 'Would you like more fish? Manolis is waiting to serve out second helpings. He's still got more barbouni on the barbecue, I believe.'

Michaelis leaned back against his own chair, drumming his fingers lightly on the table as he watched her. 'No, thanks.'

'Stavros, perhaps you would like some more fish?' She turned towards the musician, who also solemnly declined, whilst carefully avoiding having to look at Michaelis.

What on earth was the matter with the pair of them? Sara felt she would like to knock their heads together!

The succulent spit-roasted lamb that followed was a great success with all the guests. Everyone complimented the cooks, and glasses were raised to Manolis and Maria as they cleared the plates.

Sara looked round the room and found herself feeling assured that she was among good friends on this island where she planned to make her home. Nothing was going to spoil this venture. Nothing was going to make her change her mind in midstream, as she had done before.

Coffee was served on the terrace, where the light of the moon was now illuminating the tops of the mysterious hills. The guests began to say their goodbyes and drift away homewards. Stavros was one of the first to leave, followed shortly by Michaelis.

Sara, who had been saying goodbye to other guests whose cars were parked in front of the house, walked across to Michaelis's car.

He turned to look at her, one hand on the door of his Land Rover, the other swinging his keys.

'Goodbye, Sara. Thank you for a most enjoyable

evening. It's not often I get a good swim before a dinner party.'

His tone was bantering and his dark eyes were giving nothing away. She still had no idea if he actually had enjoyed being with her this evening, or if he was merely being polite. They'd spent most of the coffee time chatting to each other, but only in a perfunctory sort of way. She hadn't in any way felt she was any closer to finding out what made this fascinating man tick. Why did he hide behind this glib façade? Why did he look as if he was still suffering? And what was the unknown grudge he held against Stavros?

'I'll be reporting for duty in a couple of days,' Sara said. 'I expect it will be something of a change from being in Accident and Emergency at Moortown General Hospital.'

'We'll all try to help you settle in.' Michaelis nodded. 'Caring for patients is the same the world over, so don't worry.'

He climbed lithely into his car and started the engine. 'Goodnight, Sara.'

As she watched the sturdy vehicle sweeping off along the road in a shower of small gravel stones, she found herself wishing that the next couple of days would pass quickly.

As he drove back along the road that hugged the side of the hill on one side and skirted the sheer drop into the sea on the other, Michaelis felt himself relaxing. It was always an ordeal nowadays to join in these social gatherings. He never felt totally at ease when he was with his colleagues outside hospital. And who on earth had conceived the mad idea of inviting Stavros, of all people?

Michaelis changed down a gear to descend a steep slope. This was a part of the road that had no lights, but as he turned the corner of the hillside he was confronted by the bright illumination of Ceres town. Dear old Ceres! The place where he was born, where he was married, where he'd meant to bring up his children…

He swallowed hard as a lump rose in his throat. If only…

On impulse, he pulled over and parked outside the first taverna on the outskirts of Ceres town. The people who owned this taverna were new to the island. Nobody would involve him in idle gossip about his family. Nobody would ask questions about how he was coping on his own.

*'Ena café, parakalor,'* he said to the young man behind the deserted bar, before walking outside again and sitting at a table near the sea.

The coffee was strong and hot, searing the back of his throat as he sipped it, staring out across the bay of Ceres.

Yes, he was glad tonight was over, but he'd enjoyed being with Sara. He'd felt a certain empathy oozing out of her. She hadn't asked him demanding questions about his home life. Hadn't enquired how Krisanthe had… Again, the lump rose in his throat as he thought about his wife. How long would it be before he could lay the circumstances of her death to rest? A lifetime? It seemed like a lifetime already, and he was no nearer being able to forget that night when his beautiful Krisanthe had died.

He looked up at the bright moon and drew in his breath at the brilliance of the night sky punctuated by the tiny pinpricks of twinkling stars. There was so much beauty and happiness on this island, but he found it hard to tune into anything other than sadness. He'd tried...God knows, he'd tried! But there was so much sadness buried deep inside him...and anger. Real anger at the fact that this never should have happened. Anger directed towards...

No, he couldn't go down that road again. It was seeing Stavros again that had upset him. But kind, sympathetic Sara had put him at his ease. If he allowed himself he could be attracted to her. Yes, it was the first time he'd felt that he might open up to someone since...

The young barman had come outside and sat down on a chair. Taking out a packet of cigarettes, he offered one to Michaelis. Michaelis shook his head and stood up, saying he had to leave. He put some money on the table and climbed back into his Land Rover.

As he drove slowly around the harbour, carefully avoiding the thick knotted ropes used for tying up boats and the huge empty baskets waiting to be filled with fish, he wondered what it would have been like to be going back to his own young family instead of an empty house.

He'd noticed the warmth of the Metcalfe family when he'd been over to see them in England. And it had still been there tonight. Transported to this Greek island, they'd brought their own ambience with them. But most of all he'd felt a special kind of radiant warmth surrounding young Sara. Now not so young! She'd been utterly charming at sixteen, conscious of those unsightly teenage spots, but still managing to display her attractive, vivid personality in her conversation and the brilliant way she'd played the piano.

He changed gear as he rounded a hairpin bend on

the road up to the higher town, catching a glimpse of the bay of Ceres beneath him. The boats were still. The visiting yachts still had lights twinkling where tourists were making the most of the warm, calm evening to have a final nightcap on deck.

Yes, he remembered the sixteen-year-old Sara vividly. That vivacious smile, the sparkling lively eyes. Over the years he'd glimpsed her occasionally on holiday on the island. She'd usually been with friends, and he hadn't expected she would remember him anyway so he hadn't approached her. Especially in the days before he'd worked on his English. She would have dissolved into a fit of giggles if he'd made mistakes.

As he drove over the brow of the hill and crossed the side of the valley to the road that led to his house, he reflected that he was glad Sara hadn't changed much. She was much more beautiful now, of course, but it wasn't her beauty that had attracted him tonight so much as her personality…

He deliberately checked this line of thought as he pulled up in front of his house. He hadn't really been attracted to her, had he? Not in that physical sense that could ruin everything if he allowed himself to let down his guard.

He wasn't going to go down that road again. Not for anybody. However attractive or appealing they appeared to be!

Sara found the next two days had flown quickly by. Standing outside the hospital, she had a momentary qualm about how she would cope with this new job. Was she going to be able to adapt to a smaller hospital, to being part of a smaller team where everybody would get to know each other more intimately?

A large Land Rover was drawing up behind her in the car park. She recognised Michaelis at the wheel. He was jumping down, his face wreathed in smiles. He seemed pleased to see her. Well, that was a good start!

'You look a bit lost, Sara. How did you get here?'

'Manolis brought me round in the boat. Chloe had taken the car. She needed to go in earlier.'

'Ah, yes, we had an emergency Caesarian and Night Sister wanted Chloe to be there. They phoned me to say the delivery was successful.'

Michaelis put a hand lightly under her elbow and steered her towards the front entrance of the hospital.

'Chloe tells me you're the medical director of the hospital now,' Sara said as they walked in through the wide open doors.

Michaelis smiled. 'Not as grand as it sounds, Sara. Medical Director is a title given to me because I've agreed to be...how do you say it in English?...general dogsbody, I think! I have to co-ordinate all the services we provide in the hospital, but I also find myself sometimes unblocking the drains because the plumber has a hangover from too much ouzo the night before.'

Sara laughed. 'Sounds an interesting job—yours, I mean, not the plumber's.'

'Never a dull moment, as you English say. Come into my office and I'll give you a briefing on what you're supposed to be doing, Sara.'

Michaelis was steering her quickly through the busy reception area. Once inside his room, Sara noticed he was more relaxed.

'Coffee? I always start the day with coffee,' Michaelis said. Without waiting for an answer he poured out a couple of cups from a cafetière on his desk. 'I've got the staff well trained in the art of making my coffee. That's about the only perk of this job that I can think of.'

Michaelis leaned against the back of his leather chair and looked across the desk to where Sara was sitting, bolt upright on a wooden chair. The sign on Michaelis's desk was making her nervous. Dr Michaelis Stangos, Medical Director. Suddenly he seemed less approachable than he had the other evening.

She took a sip of her coffee and put the cup down on Michaelis's desk. 'Tell me where I'll be working in the hospital.'

Michaelis smiled and Sara felt herself relaxing again. 'You'll be working everywhere, Sara. The rule of the hospital is that we all work where we're needed at any particular time. That way we rarely have a staff shortage. There are no specialists as such, but obviously each of us has special skills. For instance my special interest is in surgery, so I spend a lot of time in the operating theatre. We've noted that you've specialised in Accident and Emergency procedures, so you'll be very useful in our reception area.'

'Reception area? But…'

'Don't be misled by the name. Everyone comes in through the main entrance and their needs are assessed by staff manning the desk. If it's an emergency the patient is immediately taken to see a doctor or nurse in the emergency area close by. I'll put you in this area initially, but not for long. You'll be expected to spend some time on the wards, as all the nurses do. All our staff say they enjoy the variety of work that this system offers.'

'Are you able to deal with any emergency here at the hospital?'

Michaelis hesitated. 'We can deal with any emergency up to the point when a patient might require specialised intensive care treatment. In that case we will do what we can before having the patient airlifted by helicopter to Rhodes or Athens. Twenty years ago there was no hospital here, just a doctor's surgery in the old pharmacy in the upper town. It was the advent of tourists that prompted the founding of our hospital. We're having to expand it all the time as demand outstrips our resources.'

'You must be very proud to be in charge here,' Sara said quietly.

Michaelis leaned forward and spread his hands palms upwards in a self-deprecating manner on the desk.

'Proud? That isn't a word that I would ever apply to myself. Sure, I'm proud of the hospital—proud to have a good team here, proud of the work we do—but I'm only a small part of the team.'

Michaelis picked up the sign on his desk and pursed his lips. 'I didn't seek to be this so-called medical director person. I was asked by the medical board if I would do the job when the last director retired. I'd been working here since medical school in Athens and, having been born on the island, I think the powers that be regarded me as a natural for the position.'

He turned his head to look across at the view from the window. Sara followed his gaze and saw the clear blue sky, the sun shining on the boats in the harbour capturing his attention.

'My elevated position hasn't made a scrap of difference to what I do here,' Michaelis continued in a faraway voice, 'except to give me more work. I've had to insist on a secretary because I can't keep up with all the paperwork on my own. I'm essentially a hands-on doctor. More than anything else this morning I'd like to be out there on the water, rounding the bay, with the wind in my sails…'

His voice trailed away. Sara smiled. For a brief moment Michaelis had reminded her of her father. He must be a very good doctor to have reached this position in the hierarchy, but it wasn't the be all [illegible] end all of his life. He was simply doing a good [illegible] to the best of his abilities, but he also had another [illegible] outside the hospital.

Michaelis looked across the desk at Sara as he recognised from her expression that she was empathising with him. This girl seemed to understand hi[illegible] ar[illegible] uncanny way, to know what he wa[illegible]self! He felt about…even when he wasn't so sure h[illegible] a strong surge of attraction tow[illegible]ner. She listened quietly to what he said, her lovely green eyes watching him as if she really cared. She was so warm, so understanding in her manner.

'You know something, Sara?' Michaelis said, suddenly becoming alert again. 'If I get half the chance of escaping today I'd like to walk over that hill over there…see, the one with the old windmills outlined against the skyline?'

Sara looked to where he was pointing and nodded. 'It looks very inviting up there. Well, you're the boss. Why don't you just go?'

Michaelis smiled, that sad, poignant smile that tore at Sara's heartstrings. 'It's the patient who's the boss.

If I'm needed here then I'll stay, but if the hospital's ticking over nicely I'll escape for a few hours.'

He hesitated, but only for a couple of seconds. 'Would you like to come with me?'

'Me?'

Michaelis grinned mischievously as he looked around the room. 'Well, there's nobody else in the room as far as I can see.'

'But what about my work?'

'I'll schedule you for a half-day off duty. We do give off duty to our nurses, you know. Would you like to come with me, if I arrange everything?'

'Well, of course... I mean, it's a beautiful day out there and...'

'Exactly!'

The door opened and a small, dark middle-aged lady neatly dressed in a black skirt and white blouse, came in with a bundle of letters which she placed on Michaelis's desk.

'*Efharisto*—thank you, Panayota,' Michaelis said, and his secretary smiled before going back into her office.

'Though why I should want to thank Panayota for my paperwork, I don't know,' Michaelis added, picking up the first envelope from the top of the pile and frowning before putting it down again. 'My least favourite job—checking the morning post.'

Reaching for the phone, he told Sara he would alert the sister in the emergency area of reception to the fact that the new staff nurse was on her way down. He spoke rapidly in Greek into the phone before cutting the connection.

Standing up, he held out his hand across the desk.

'Good luck, Sara! I'll see you at the end of the morning.'

As Sara clasped Michaelis's outstretched hand she imagined she could feel a certain strength flowing from him. And something else she could barely define. The sense of excitement at being in touch with his skin was definitely arousing her senses, and the faint scent of his aftershave was decidedly unnerving.

As she took away her hand it seemed to tingle with a sensual current. It was time she got down to some real work and put some distance between Michaelis and herself!

As the door closed behind Sara, Michaelis leaned back against his chair and took a deep breath. He was already having second thoughts about being so impulsive. It was everything he'd decided was out of bounds to him.

Yes, he'd often dated women, but only because they were amusing or interesting and didn't arouse the slightest emotion inside him. His rule was to ensure that he and his date had a mutually enjoyable time without any involvement, so long as the feeling was mutual and nobody was going to get hurt. If he'd planned to be celibate he would have become a monk!

But in the whole of his life he'd never gone out with a married or engaged woman. They were totally taboo as far as he was concerned. He'd simply enjoyed a brief fling occasionally with unattached women who'd made it obvious they wanted to go out with him.

But with Sara he could already feel that the situation was completely different. He was desperately attracted to her. She was stirring up emotions that had lain dormant for years. Emotions that he wanted to keep contained within himself for the rest of his life. He didn't want to break his own safety rules. He didn't want to lay himself wide open to someone who could break his heart and leave him scarred for life...as Krisanthe had done.

He swallowed hard as he gripped the sides of his seat. He'd been weak just now. He'd been impulsive, moved by that charming smile, the way Sara turned him on when she crossed her legs in front of him and leaned back, displaying a figure that curved in all the right places. She was obviously trying to look demure but unconsciously giving out signals that she was a very sensual and attractive woman.

Well, Sara needn't know how he felt. She was a level-headed person. If he kept control of his emotions neither of them would get hurt. He'd only asked her out for a walk over the hill, for God's sake!

With a sigh, he picked up the first envelope from the top of the pile on his desk.

Sara walked past the reception desk and made her way over to the area marked 'Emergencies'. A small Greek sister in a dark blue uniform dress hurried over to meet her. She looked harassed as she handed Sara a large package.

'I'm Sister Eleni. There are two uniforms in there for you, Sara. I do hope they fit. We only got your measurements a couple of days ago. You can change out of your own clothes in the staff cloakroom, but be quick because there's an emergency patient on the way.'

The cloakroom was small, and was obviously used as a storeroom as well as having a couple of loos and a washbasin. Sara had to step over packets of toilet rolls and soap to reach the area where she could undress. Hanging her jeans and blouse on a peg, she pulled the white uniform dress over her head. It wasn't a perfect fit, but it would suffice if she tightened the belt she'd brought with her. Everywhere she went she took her own hospital belt and badge. It made her feel at home and more efficient at the same time.

Hurrying out into the emergency area, she saw Eleni hovering beside a patient on the trolley that had just been wheeled in.

'Ah, Sara, come over here. Help me get this patient on to the examination couch. Andonis will be with us soon. I bleeped him a few minutes ago.' Eleni lowered her voice. 'The patient has gastric problems, I was told over the phone.'

'Easy does it,' Sara said, as she and the sister rolled the patient gently from the trolley to the examination couch.

The middle-aged Greek woman groaned. Her arms remained clutching her stomach, giving a clear sign of where she felt most pain. She was muttering in Greek. Sara tried hard to get the gist of what she was saying. Her own Greek had improved over the years she had been coming out here to Ceres, reinforced by the Greek classes she'd taken back home in England, but she still struggled if someone was speaking quickly or quietly. Eleni had been called away to another patient across the room—a screaming child who was refusing to be examined.

Sara would have to deal with this emergency on her own. Swiftly she drew the curtains around the cubicle and leaned over her patient.

*'Posseleni?'* Sara asked gently. 'What's your name?'

The woman's anguished eyes stared up at Sara. 'Diana…'

Sara listened carefully as Diana told her about the terrible pain in her stomach and back. It had started in her back early this morning, but now… 'Aagh!'

The woman clutched her stomach as Sara began to help remove her outer garments. The Greeks insisted it was still technically winter here on Ceres, and in spite of the warm sunshine Diana was in her warm winter clothes and there were several layers. Removing a huge sweater and a couple of blouses, Sara began to form her own diagnosis. Her patient was obviously overweight, and when Sara pulled back the large blouse covering her stomach she had very little doubt.

The rustling of the curtain behind her told her that help had arrived. She turned, expecting to see Andonis.

Michaelis was shrugging on a white coat as he came across the cubicle.

'Andonis is treating a gastric patient who's been haemorrhaging so I've come to answer his emergency call instead. I told you I had to fill in everywhere, didn't I?'

He glanced down at the patient, his eyes narrowing as he took in the whole scenario.

'Eleni told me our patient has gastric problems, but…' He raised his eyes.

Sara's eyes met Michaelis's across the patient.

'More obstetric than gastric, I think. Don't you?' Sara said quietly.

Michaelis nodded before speaking quickly in Greek

to their patient. Sara noticed he was enunciating carefully so that she, herself, would have no difficulty in understanding what he was saying.

She'd worked through the majority of medical terms she would encounter, and she recognised from the brief discussion between Michaelis and his patient that Diana hadn't had a period for a long time. But then, their patient said, this was understandable as she'd now gone into the menopause. The lack of periods had nothing to do with her stomach ache, and would Michaelis please get a move on and give her something to take away the pain?

Michaelis was now explaining that he was going to examine Diana 'down below'. Diana grimaced, but allowed Sara to prepare her for the examination.

Scrubbing up at the sink, Michaelis told Sara that he always found it hard to treat a patient who'd known him all his life. Patients like Diana couldn't grasp the fact that he was a fully qualified, experienced doctor and there was no need for them to be embarrassed when he examined them. And Diana, at the age of forty-five, had never had a baby, and probably never had an internal medical examination in her life, so she was understandably apprehensive.

Sara held Diana's legs gently but firmly in lithotomy position so that Michaelis could examine their patient per vagina.

'The cervix is almost fully dilated, Sara,' Michaelis reported quietly.

Diana let out a piercing scream. 'What's happening? What's happening, Michaelis? I can't bear the pain… I can't, I can't…'

'I'll give Diana some pain relief. Sara, would you

like to tell Diana what's happening?' Michaelis said as he began to set up the entonox machine.

'Diana, you haven't got gastric problems. You're going to have a baby,' Sara said gently as she held her patient's hand.

Diana was sweating profusely. Sara wiped her face with cool gauze and held her head so that she could take a sip of water.

'What did you say? Oh, this pain's coming again. I need to go to the toilet. I need…'

Michaelis clamped the entonox mask over his patient's face. 'Breathe into the mask, Diana. This will help the pain. Breathe deeply… No, don't push down—don't push down… You're having a baby and at this particular moment you mustn't push. Do you understand?'

Their patient's eyes above the mask had registered amazement at first, but now appeared calmer as the gas and air flowing through the mask took effect.

'Cervix is fully dilated, Sara,' Michaelis said. 'How's the fetal heartbeat?'

Sara had been checking the baby's heartbeat with a Pinard's stethoscope and she reported that it was full and steady. She was reassured that this unexpected baby wasn't suffering in any way, but she would feel nothing but relief when it had been safely delivered.

Eleni had come in to see what was happening. 'Don't you think we should take Diana along to the delivery suite, Michaelis?'

'Both rooms are in use at the moment. I just checked. Besides, Diana will be more comfortable here than being wheeled along the corridor. Can we have some sterile gowns please, Sister? And, Sara, swab the vulval and perineal areas when you're gowned and masked.'

Sara put on the sterile gown that Eleni handed to her. She reached for a bottle of antiseptic solution and swabbed the areas most vital to the baby's delivery.

'The baby's head's crowning,' Michaelis said. He raised his head. 'Diana, you mustn't push. Breathe like this...'

Michaelis gave a brief demonstration of how to pant, glancing over at Sara to make sure she reinforced his instructions.

'Like this, Diana.' Sara panted slowly to demonstrate the easiest way of avoiding pushing at this crucial stage.

'For someone who's never been to an antenatal class you've caught on quickly,' Sara murmured in English, more to herself than her patient.

She squeezed her patient's hand and reverted to Greek again. 'Good, very good, Diana... Yes, don't stop yet... Now you can stop. You see, when the baby's head is waiting to be born it's important not to push it out too quickly. The head and the face of the baby must be born slowly.'

'I can't believe this, Nurse,' Diana said, clinging on to her hand. 'It's like a dream. I didn't know I was going to have a baby. I've always wanted a baby, but it never happened and so— Aagh, can I push now?'

'Yes, you can push now, Diana. Michaelis is holding your baby's head carefully. He's made sure that the umbilical cord—the lifeline between you and the baby—isn't round baby's neck, so now...yes, push. The shoulders are out now, and...'

As Sara heard the final swoosh of the baby's body

slithering out of the birth canal she gave a sigh of relief.

'Your baby's safely here, Diana.'

'I can hear that,' the new mother said, tears of joy streaming down her face as she listened to the lusty crying of the newborn infant.

'It's a boy, Diana.' Michaelis smiled, wrapping the slippery little body in a dressing sheet and handing the precious bundle over to the proud mother.

'I can't believe it. I can't believe it… Oh, I love you so much,' Diana told her baby, holding him so tightly that Sara checked to see she wasn't squeezing the tiny little mite too hard.

'Somebody get my husband—get Iannis, please. But give him a Metaxa brandy before you break the news. I don't want him fainting on me!'

'Diana, we're going to move you to the delivery suite,' Michaelis said. 'You and the baby need to be checked over. Everything's fine, but we haven't finished with you yet. I'll get a message to Iannis, don't worry.'

'Iannis is going to be so thrilled. He always wanted a son. Twenty years we've been married, and it just didn't happen. Thank you, Michaelis, and thank you, Nurse. You were wonderful! I never thought that…'

Sara looked at Michaelis as Diana was wheeled away, still counting her blessings and saying she was the happiest woman in the world.

'It's always a great feeling when you make a patient happy, isn't it, Sara?' Michaelis said gently.

Sara could feel tears pricking at the back of her eyes as she listened to the gentle tones in Michaelis's voice. After all her years of training and experience in the medical profession, delivering a new baby still

made her feel emotional. But she felt even more so with this new birth, because she'd shared the experience with Michaelis. He was a big man, tall in stature, muscular and athletic, but with a gentle heart. A vulnerable heart. Possibly a heart that had been broken?

He leaned towards her now, his hand reaching out to touch her but at the last moment withdrawing. 'I've got to get back to my work.'

She watched as he turned and moved away quickly.

She felt a moment of panic. He hadn't mentioned what was happening this afternoon—if anything was to happen. Perhaps he'd changed his mind or he was too busy.

'Michaelis, are you going to be able to get away this afternoon?' she heard herself calling after him.

Put like that it sounded so brazen. She felt the colour rising in her cheeks as Michaelis turned round.

'I've already scheduled you for a half-day this afternoon, Sara. Unless something else comes up I'll be able to get away as well.'

His expression was totally enigmatic. After the excited, effervescent manner he'd adopted when they were discussing the outcome of the unexpected birth, it was something of an anticlimax.

'Sara!'

Eleni's voice brought her up sharp. She'd only just started work here and she was already planning a half-day with Michaelis, worrying about whether this was a good idea or not—for either of them. A couple of hours' work would bring her back to reality.

# CHAPTER THREE

IT WAS a steep climb to the top of the hill where the four old windmills stood, rooted in the hard granite rock. Now no longer needed, they had withstood years of battering from the winter winds and rain to remain lasting monuments of a bygone era.

As Sara arrived at the last windmill on the skyline she sat down on the grass, breathing deeply to stop herself from panting.

'A good place to take a rest and have our picnic lunch, I think,' Michaelis said, kneeling down on the grass beside her.

Sara smiled up at him. 'Thank goodness for that! That last bit of the hill was almost a slope too far for me. I'm not used to playing at mountain goats.'

Michaelis laughed as he reached into his rucksack and began pulling out intriguing-looking paper packets. 'Oh, you'll soon get used to it. Just look at all this food! Our hospital cook has given me enough for a whole family. I hope you're hungry.'

'Starving! It's been a long morning.'

As Sara bit into a delicious salami sandwich her mind flashed back over the events that had brought her up to this high place for lunch. When she'd left home with Manolis in the boat this morning she'd never imagined so much would happen. First the poignant, unexpected birth, followed by several more minor emergencies, and then, just before she'd been

going to come off duty, a dear little boy with a broken leg that she'd had to set in plaster.

Everyone else who knew about plastering a leg had gone to lunch, and Sara had volunteered so that the little boy wouldn't have to wait any longer. She remembered, with a pang of sadness, how her little patient had cried when she'd told him he mustn't ride his bike again until the plaster came off. It was so difficult to explain things like that to a tiny tot with a brand-new bike.

But now the best part of her day—an expedition over the hills with Michaelis. He'd accepted her explanation about why she'd been late coming off duty and he hadn't been impatient with her. It was probably because he was a true professional—as she always liked to think she was herself.

She propped her back against a large rock as she turned to look at Michaelis.

'You know, I feel a bit guilty only working one morning on my first day.'

'Don't worry. We'll crack the whip in the days to come, I promise you. Anyway, we can't complain about the work we got out of you this morning. I'm particularly thrilled that Diana has had a baby after all these years. I remember going to her wedding twenty years ago. The whole island turns out for weddings, by the way. You don't need to be invited. The more, the merrier—and, believe me, wedding celebrations get merrier and merrier as the wine flows and the dancing starts.'

Michaelis paused. 'Talking of which—wine, that is—I've got a bottle somewhere at the bottom here. Retsina OK? The bottle is small enough to fit into my rucksack but not so small that we'll feel deprived.

I've also got a bottle of water to quench our thirst when we need it, which we will soon enough.'

Sara watched as Michaelis snapped off the top of the sturdy brown-coloured retsina bottle with a bottle opener. He handed her a steel cup and she took a tentative sip. She'd always found retsina a bit too strong in the past, but it tasted delicious now that she was really thirsty and she assumed she would easily walk off the effects of the alcohol content during the next few hours.

'Tell me some more about Diana,' Sara said as she wedged her steel cup in a cleft in the rock. 'Thanks.'

She took another sandwich from the packet that Michaelis was holding out towards her. This one was filled with feta cheese, olives and tomato, and it tasted delicious.

Michaelis leaned back against the rock beside her. 'Well, as I told you, Diana and Iannis have been married for twenty years. They both come from big families and it was common knowledge that they were longing to start a family of their own. I remember after five years there was some whispering and conjecture going on among their friends and relatives about the fact that Diana and Iannis still hadn't had a child. I'd just qualified and returned from Athens to work in the hospital, and I fully expected they would come in for checks on their fertility.'

'And did they?'

'No, they didn't. People stopped asking them when they were going to start a family and they never mentioned it any more.'

Sara nodded. 'Some couples seem as if they don't want to admit there is a problem that might be sorted out with medical help.'

'Exactly! Well, they just seemed to accept that they were a childless couple after a while. This morning Diana told me that when her periods stopped she assumed it was the menopause, and when she started to get fatter she thought it was middle-age spread. She's been overweight for a few years now, and she was actually carrying the baby high in her midriff so it just seemed as if her waist was thickening. When the distressing pains started, early today, she naturally thought she was having some awful problem in her stomach.'

'Did you manage to contact Diana's husband?'

Michaelis smiled. 'Iannis was…how do you say it in English?…gob-pushed?'

Sara laughed. 'Gob-smacked. So, did someone give him a Metaxa brandy?'

'When Iannis arrived at the hospital he was already…three sheets to…?'

'Three sheets to the wind,' Sara supplied laughingly. 'You'll be able to pass yourself off as an Englishman soon.'

Michaelis grinned. 'That'll be the day.'

He jumped to his feet and held out a hand towards Sara. 'I think we should get moving. It's quite a long walk over to the next bay, and daylight soon fades at this time of the year.'

Sara took hold of Michaelis's outstretched hand. As his fingers clasped hers she felt a sensation of unreality. Here she was on the top of this panoramic hill with someone she'd only met a few times, and yet she felt as if she'd known Michaelis all her life. There was already an affinity between them, a rapport that didn't need words to express itself.

She walked behind him along the narrow, single

track goats' path. It petered out in places, but Michaelis knew in which direction to make his way between the sparse grass and wild spring flowers. She stopped to admire a particularly beautiful white flower shaped like an orchid. Michaelis told her the name in Greek, but she had difficulty pronouncing it and planned to look it up in her dictionary when she got home, so that she could write it down.

A mother goat on the hillside called to her offspring, admonishing the little kid for straying too far away. Sara paused to watch the goat scurrying down the hillside towards the now frightened kid, who was making an alarmingly strident cry for such a tiny animal. As soon as they were reunited the kid latched on to its mother and began suckling hungrily.

Starting out again, she saw that Michaelis was waiting for her, a gentle smile on his lips.

'Isn't Mother Nature wonderful?' he said softly. 'It never ceases to amaze me how similar animals are to human beings in behaviour.'

Sara nodded. 'We can put on airs and graces and pretend to be superior, but at the end of the day the most basic things in life, like being part of a family, having a mother you can love and trust—'

She broke off, unnerved by the sad expression that had suddenly clouded Michaelis's face.

'Go on,' he said, his voice husky with emotion. 'I want to hear it from someone who's part of a loving family. It's what I believe, but I like to know that I'm not biased.'

He crouched down, patting the grass at the side of the path before taking out a bottle of water and pouring out two cupfuls.

She joined him on the grass as she took a sip of

water. 'Like you, I believe that family is terribly important. It's where you come from, where you go back to when you need to retreat from the world and lick your wounds, isn't it?'

Michaelis remained silent, sipping his water, staring out across the rocky valley towards the blue sea that stretched on one side towards the Turkish coast and on the other towards the island of Rhodes.

'I left my family when I got married,' Michaelis said quietly, after a few minutes. 'I intended to start my own family. But when…when it didn't happen, I didn't feel I could go back to the family home and pretend everything was just as it had been before I'd married. Oh, my mother and father begged me to return, but I didn't want their pity.'

Sara held her breath as she listened to the hardening of Michaelis's tone.

'But don't you think everybody needs a little pity when they've suffered?' she said gently. 'A little sympathy never did anybody any harm…'

'No!' Michaelis gazed down at Sara with dark, melancholic eyes. 'When Krisanthe died I told my parents I didn't want sympathy. Not if it meant them prying into my affairs. Trying to find out why…'

He paused for a moment before continuing. 'My mother wanted to know too many details about my marriage. She suspected…she suspected far too much. You know what mothers are like.'

Sara nodded. 'They've got too much intuition. You can't hide anything from them, can you?'

'Exactly! Oh, Sara!'

Michaelis drew in his breath as he thought how he would have welcomed sympathy from Sara at that dark period of his life. Here she was, listening to him telling her only half the story, keeping the tragic details to himself, and she wasn't asking any questions. If she ever did start to enquire, as most people usually did, then…

'Let's walk,' Sara said briskly, brushing the dust from her jeans as she stood up.

She recognised that she'd begun something that had touched on a raw nerve for Michaelis. There was obviously some deep mystery surrounding the death of his wife. Something he wanted to hide even from…indeed, especially from…his own mother.

She moved quickly off along the path, which was well defined now. Behind her she could hear Michaelis strapping on his rucksack, followed by the heavy thud of his trainers on the rocky path.

She turned round as he caught up with her. 'You'd better lead. I'm much slower than you and I'll hold up the pace.'

He moved to stand beside her on the narrow path. She looked up at him and he put his hands on her shoulders, drawing her against him.

'Thanks, Sara.'

She could feel the beating of his heart. 'Thanks for what?'

'For…for being here. For listening and not—'

He broke off and moved away to begin walking in front of her again. She followed as quickly as she could, but he was now setting a furious pace, only occasionally looking round to check that Sara wasn't finding it too demanding.

Michaelis had reached the top of the hill that looked down on the bay. Sara arrived, breathless, shortly after him, and gazed down at the picturesque scene below her.

'It's such a beautiful view from up here! The bay is absolutely deserted.'

'It always is in the winter and the early spring. People start coming out here when the weather warms up. It's a great place for swimming in the summer. There's sand at the bottom of the bay, which is easy on the feet, and it's not too far to swim out to the little chapel over there on the island.'

Sara shielded her eyes from the slanting sun as her eyes followed in the direction Michaelis was pointing.

'I'd like to swim out there one day,' she said. 'But I didn't bring a swimsuit today...and the water's probably too cold anyway,' she added hurriedly.

'I didn't notice the cold a couple of days ago, in Nymborio Bay,' Michaelis said quietly, almost as if he was testing her.

'You were intent on saving a life, so I don't suppose you thought about yourself very much.'

Michaelis was looking up at the sun, which was beginning to dip down in the sky. 'I'll bring you here for swimming one day, when we have more time.'

Sara's heart gave a little hop, skip and jump at the thought that Michaelis was warming towards her enough to want to see her again in an off duty situation. She sensed he was a very deep character. He didn't wear his heart on his sleeve, and there must have been so many problems in his marriage which had ended so tragically that it had scarred him for life.

She wasn't going to pry, but she hoped that by listening she could maybe help to heal a few wounds.

They scrambled their way down the steep, zigzagging, stony path that led to the deserted beach. A couple of goats, wandering along the shore, scattered nervously as they approached. Michaelis offered them a couple of the remaining sandwiches from his rucksack. They ate them greedily and then proceeded to follow on behind.

'Goats will eat anything,' Michaelis said. 'I don't usually feed them, except in the winter or the early spring. In summer they can fend for themselves. They'll soon leave us alone when we ignore them.'

The goats had already moved further away, to begin their climb back up the hillside.

Michaelis put down his rucksack on the sand at the water's edge and sat down. Sara joined him, easing off her shoes and socks. Rolling up her jeans to the knee, she plunged her feet into the sea. As the initial cold shock subsided she found the experience was soothing and energising at the same time.

'The water's not too cold for swimming, Michaelis. Maybe we could...' Her voice trailed away.

Michaelis was already stripping off, and suddenly Sara had no difficulty in following suit. This was no time to be coy, when the sparkling sea was exerting its magical, magnetic force towards her.

As a child, she'd never been able to resist the call of the sea. She would always run down to the shoreline and be soaking wet before the rest of the family had even set off down the beach.

As she stripped down to her underwear she caught a glimpse of Michaelis's dark, suntanned body diving into the sea and tried desperately to erase the picture from her mind. She was trying to put herself into professional mode as far as their semi-nudity was concerned, but the sight of Michaelis's athletically muscular frame disappearing beneath the sparkling blue surface of the water wasn't something she would be able to forget in a hurry.

Wading out to a waist-high depth, her toes revelling in the soft sand beneath them, she felt that her near-nakedness was of absolutely no consequence in the grand scheme of her life at the moment. She felt completely at ease now, and the touch of the cold water on her skin was having the effect of damping down the spasms of erotic excitement she'd felt when she'd glimpsed Michaelis diving in.

He was already halfway out in the bay now, using that strong, fast crawl he'd adopted when he was life-saving Jonathan and Jane with Manolis the other evening. She followed him, keeping some way behind. The crawl had never been her favourite stroke, but she did a strong breast stroke.

It soon became obvious that Michaelis was making his way towards the tiny island at the entrance to the bay. Sara wondered if he was planning to go up to the little church. Raising her head from the water, she saw him stop short of the island, holding on to a large rock.

She trod water close by and watched him. He was holding his head backwards, his eyes closed, bathing in the warm rays of the late-afternoon sunshine.

Suddenly Michaelis opened his eyes and saw her close by. 'Come and rest by this rock, Sara. I don't think we should go on to the island. We're probably not suitably dressed for church today.'

Sara laughed, getting a mouthful of water as she did so, but feeling her whole body relax as she reached the rock and took hold of a small section. Slowly she began to take deep breaths, to re-establish a breathing pattern after her exertions in the water. It felt so wonderful to be suspended here in time with Michaelis.

He reached out his hand and took hold of hers. 'You're colder than me, Sara. Do you feel OK?'

'I'm fine! Enjoying myself!' She licked the salt from her lips.

Michaelis's eyes registered his concern. 'I think we should start off back before you become too cold.'

'In a minute. It's so peaceful here, and so…so out of this world.'

Michaelis moved closer and suddenly his arms were around her. She looked up at him, revelling in the sensuous excitement that coursed through her veins as their upper bodies touched. But it was only a brief moment. Michaelis, as if sensing that he might be overstepping the bounds of propriety, moved back to his own section of the rock. But the sensuality lingered on.

Sara pushed herself off from the rock quickly. The effort of propelling herself through the water helped to dampen down her renewed excitement. The brief touch of Michaelis's body against her own had totally unnerved her. She realised with a pang that she'd wanted more…oh, so much more!

Michaelis was swimming beside her now. She wondered what he would have done if she'd encouraged that brief embrace. Would he have thought her forward, a push-over, just one of the many girls who were attracted to him? But if she'd given him a sign that she wanted him, would he have held her closer, would he have…?

She gave an involuntary shiver as an exciting vision of herself and Michaelis making love in the water presented itself. She was shocked to realise that she could even think of something like that when she'd spent so little time with him. But there was something about Michaelis that was oh, so different from the other men she'd known in her life. And today the strong, magnetic pull of the sea coupled with this new surging interest in Michaelis was giving her a light-headed feeling of unreality.

'You're shivering, Sara. How do you feel?'

Michaelis, swimming slowly by her side, sounded deeply concerned.

Oh, if you only knew how I felt! Sara thought. If she only dared tell him! But how would he react? He'd started that wonderful embrace and then backed off as if scared she would reciprocate and come on too strong, possibly demanding more than he wanted to give.

Michaelis raised his head out of the water. Not far to the shore now. He wanted to get Sara back on dry land because she was looking decidedly strange. Probably exhausted by the events of the day. He shouldn't have suggested the swim after their long walk. It had tired her too much. And why on earth he'd given in to his basic instincts and put his arms around her like that he couldn't think!

Yes, she'd looked beautiful in the water, so desirable, like a tiny mermaid who'd lost her way and become washed up near the shore. That lovely soft brown hair, glistening in the sunlight, simply waiting for him to run his fingers through, her pale smooth skin just asking to be caressed…

He drew in his breath. He was in deep trouble here. Deep, deep trouble! Sara was affecting him more than he'd anticipated. Yes, she stirred his male instincts and he wanted to make love with her. But that in itself was perfectly normal. What was disturbing was that it wasn't just his physical self that was affected. It was his whole being. His entire body, mind and spirit, was becoming enslaved by this slip of a girl swimming beside him.

And, from her reaction, it seemed that he'd probably frightened her off with his awkward, impromptu, spur-of-the-moment advance. He remembered the way she'd started swimming back towards the shore, her face set in an impossibly determined expression. He'd hoped for some kind of response, but now, swimming beside her in the cold sea, he was glad Sara *hadn't* responded.

Because if she had he would have begun to caress her lovely body, would have held her so hard against him, and then…

He checked that line of thought even as it arose. Had Sara any idea what she was doing to him? This wasn't what he'd planned when he'd decided to go for an innocent swim. He'd never set out today to become so involved. He had to get himself in check before his emotions carried him away…but how?

He moved forward quickly, to reach the shore before Sara did. Turning round, he held out his hand to help her out of the water.

Sara took hold of Michaelis's hand, and then leaned on him as he led her out of the water.

'Phew! I feel exhausted.' Sara flung herself down on the shore, not even noticing the tiny pebbles sticking into her skin.

Michaelis picked up his cotton overshirt and handed it to her. 'Get dry, Sara. You can't do much about your underwear, but you'll feel warmer as soon as your skin isn't so wet. Here! Put my sweater on when you've dried yourself.'

'What about you?'

'I'm tougher than you are.'

Sara stopped shivering as she patted herself dry with Michaelis's shirt. The sensually disturbing scent of his aftershave and a pure animal maleness was deeply unnerving as the fibres of the shirt rubbed across her body.

Michaelis was behaving like the perfect gentleman. His back towards her, he was shrugging himself into his jeans and the spare tee shirt he'd extricated from the bottom of his rucksack. She didn't dare to enquire whether he was dry. The atmosphere was too heavily charged with eroticism as it was.

How could she have thought she could swim like that with Michaelis and remain cool, calm and collected? Looking at Michaelis now that they were both fully dressed, she, at his insistence, wearing his huge dark blue fisherman's jersey that reached almost to her knees, she experienced an overwhelming desire to rush into his arms and beg him to hold her.

So what was holding her back? She'd never even contemplated making the first move with a man before, but with Michaelis it was different. He looked at this moment as if he was a scared little boy who'd committed some naughty act which made him expect to be told off. Was he worried about the way he'd put his arms around her in the water?

Maybe she should reassure him that the reason she'd set off back to the shore so quickly was because she didn't trust her own emotions. Impulsively, she took a step forward and put both her hands on his waist. Moving them around to his back, she leaned her head against his chest.

'You don't mind if I warm my hands, do you?' she said quietly, her heart beating so hard she was sure Michaelis would hear it as she leaned against him.

Raising her eyes to his, she saw the look of amazement on his face. She was being too forward! She would surely frighten him off. He would think she was one of those pushy females who…

Slowly, his surprised expression turned to a look of sheer delight. Slowly, he bent his head and kissed her full on the lips. She had to stand on tiptoe to meet his kiss, but she missed none of the full impact of his sensuous, sexy mouth. Slowly his lips moved over hers, then gently, oh so gently, as her lips parted, she felt their mouths blending together. She could taste the salt of the sea on his tongue as she clung to him, revelling in the strong, muscular sensations of his caressing arms.

For a few moments time ceased to exist. They were two primeval beings, clinging to each other on a deserted beach. But even as Sara gave an involuntary sigh of ecstatic delight she could feel Michaelis pulling away from her.

He was gazing down at her, his eyes searching her face as if he needed to be reassured.

She looked up and smiled. He returned her smile, but his eyes were giving nothing away. She wondered if he'd been as deeply touched as she had when they were embracing. The kiss, the touch of his lips…

'We ought to go, Sara. The daylight is fading.'

'Yes—yes, of course.'

She was glad Michaelis hadn't felt it necessary to explain why he'd embraced her again when she had supposedly simply been warming her hands. He must know it had only been a ploy to move their relationship on further.

And, if he did, had she frightened him off? As a full-blooded man he'd responded to physical advances, but she had the feeling that was all he was interested in. A brief moment of sensuality and then it was time to get back to normal, as if nothing had happened between them.

But as she walked behind him, up the path on the opposite side of the bay from the one they'd descended earlier that afternoon, she could feel that things weren't normal. Their relationship would never be the same after this. She didn't know where it was heading, but she would love to go further and further until…

'Sara, are you OK back there?'

She looked at the spot higher up the path where Michaelis was standing, bathed in the orange glare of the setting sun, one foot poised on a rock. Her heart turned over as she reflected that he looked like a Greek god come down from Mount Olympus.

'I'm fine.'

'Good. Very soon we'll be going over the top of this hill and making our way down into the next bay, where my parents live. The path goes in front of their house so I should call in to see them for a few minutes. Will you come with me? It shouldn't take long.'

'Of course I'll come with you. I'd be delighted to meet your parents.'

Michaelis turned away and resumed his trek up the hillside. This was definitely going too far! Taking Sara to meet his parents! He could have taken the higher path and avoided their house today. But, no, something inside was driving him on. He was enjoying his time with Sara. He didn't want it to end. He wanted to feel that he would see her again…and, yes, he wanted to see the light of approval in his mother's eyes.

Now this was really getting serious! He should have checked the idea when it had arisen back there in the water. He'd fully intended to avoid seeing his parents today. He'd never taken a girlfriend to meet them before. Would they think he was making a statement about Sara? Saying that they might be going to settle down? Because nothing was further from the truth.

Sara was simply a very nice girl who was fun to be with. He hadn't lost his heart to her and he had no desire to move their relationship any further along…

Michaelis stopped in the middle of the path, ostensibly to wait until Sara could catch up with him. Turning round, he watched her picking her way over the rough stones and his heart seemed to turn over. Why did he feel like this about her? It was no use pretending to himself that he could contain these strong emotions she was stirring deep inside him.

Sara looked up and smiled. 'Are we nearly at the top?'

She sounded out of breath. Michaelis stepped back down the path to meet her. 'We're almost there. Here, take my hand.'

Sara clasped his strong, warm hand, the sensitive fingers wrapping themselves around hers reassuringly. She felt strength flowing through her again as Michaelis helped her up the last section of the uphill path.

They stood together, side by side, still holding hands, at the top of the hill, looking down first into the bay where they'd swum and then into the new bay, this one completely different. Even from this height Sara could see dear little houses dotted along the waterside, tiny pots of geraniums outlining each section of property where wooden tables and chairs had been placed for the meals the families enjoyed in the open air under the vine-entwined, slatted wooden shades. And on the water of the bay small boats were bathed in the slanting orange rays of the late-afternoon sun.

'It looks like a toy village from up here! Which one is your parents' house?'

'You can't see it yet.' Michaelis unclasped his hand from Sara's and moved to the edge of the hillside to point further along the valley. 'Their house is round that corner. They came to live here when we all left home. Our family house was in the upper town.'

Sara's eyes followed where Michaelis was pointing to a conglomeration of pastel-coloured houses clinging to the hillside at the head of the valley.

'We lived at the very top, near the castle.'

Shielding her eyes from the glare of the sun, now low in the sky, Sara tried to make out the house that Michaelis was indicating, but it was too difficult for her, being so far away. 'Did your parents come here after you married, Michaelis?'

He drew in his breath. 'Not until after my wife died. My sister was already living in Athens. She teaches in the university. And my two brothers are doctors in America. That was when my parents wanted me to go home again…but I couldn't.' He sighed. 'I simply couldn't. So I sold my little house in the upper town and bought myself a house up there, on the other side of the valley.'

Sara looked across the valley to see a white stone building completely on its own. There was a church higher up the hill, but apart from that there was no other habitation.

She nodded. 'You wanted to be alone,' she said quietly.

'Yes, it was simpler that way. I was looking for—' He broke off, as if searching for words.

'Peace?' Sara said gently.

Michaelis gave her a sad smile. 'Possibly. I don't know. We'd better go down before it gets dark.'

Sara stood in front of the small, neat, flower-bedecked whitewashed cottage beside the water and waited to be invited inside. She was feeling apprehensive about meeting Michaelis's parents. He'd told her they would only stay a few minutes. It was simply a courtesy call. As she waited for Michaelis to reappear she glanced down at her clothes and shuddered to think what kind of a first impression she would make.

Probably first and last! Because Michaelis's parents would be sure to wonder what kind of scruffy apparition he'd dredged up from the bottom of the sea!

Hastily, Sara pulled off Michaelis's sweater and dived into her bag for a comb. She could feel that her hair had dried to a salt-encrusted mess, sitting on the top of her head like a doormat.

'Would you like to come in, Sara?' Michaelis asked from the doorway. 'I've explained that we can't stay long.

Quickly she handed Michaelis his sweater, before running her hand over her hair to flatten it still further.

It was cosy and warm inside the small living room. The heat from the sun during the day, combined with the heat now given off by the small lights burning in the corners of the room, gave it an ambience that appealed to Sara.

Michaelis's mother smiled as Michaelis introduced her to Sara, but it was a weary smile that seemed to question why her son had brought a girlfriend to the house. Was she a significant girlfriend, or just someone he'd picked up to amuse himself with for a while?

'*Kalispera*—good evening,' Sara said in a polite tone.

'You can speak English,' the other woman replied. 'My husband used to work on the boats and I went with him on some of his trips. We spent a year in England before our children were born, when my husband was working on the docks at Liverpool. But we came home to Ceres for the birth of my first son. Your name is Sara, yes? And I am Irini. Would you like a drink? Tea, coffee, ouzo?'

'Brandy for Sara, I think, Mother,' Michaelis said. 'She's been swimming and the water was very cold.'

Irini looked shocked. 'Swimming in March!' She tut-tutted her disapproval as she asked Michaelis to reach up on the shelf for some five-star Metaxa.

The door opened and a tall, stocky man came in. Sara would have recognised Michaelis's father anywhere. He had the same imposing stature, slightly stooped now, but still impressive. His face was still handsome, in a hard, experience-roughened way, in spite of the deep wrinkles that were carved indelibly through it. His hair was almost black, interspersed with swathes of white.

Irini turned to look at her husband. 'Michaelis has brought a friend to see us. Sotiris, this is Sara.'

'*Yassoo*—hello.' Sotiris held out his hand solemnly, before looking at his son and speaking rapidly in Greek.

Michaelis replied quickly as he placed the Metaxa bottle on the table along with three glasses. Irini, apparently, had declined a drink. Michaelis poured out two large measures for his father and himself, and one small glass which he gave to Sara.

The fiery liquid scorched her throat as she sipped it.

She looked up at Michaelis, who still seemed strangely uneasy about something. 'You were right to prescribe this, Doctor,' she said, smiling. 'It certainly warms from the inside outwards.'

The two men laughed and Irini gave a smile.

Michaelis put his glass down on the table. 'We have to go. It's getting dark and I have to escort Sara home.'

'Where does the young lady live?' his father asked.

'Nymborio Bay. I'm going to take a taxi from—'

'No, no! You can take my boat. It will be much quicker.'

Sotiris put down his glass and made towards the door.

Sara followed, pausing to say goodbye to Michaelis's mother.

'You must come again when you have time to stay longer,' Irini said in her careful, charmingly accented English.

Sara noticed that more warmth had crept into Irini's dark eyes. The smile on her lips now was much more genuine. So maybe she'd passed the first test! The

Greek brandy had warmed her, but the short experience had been a strain.

As she went out into the gathering dusk Sara felt that Michaelis's family was a real enigma. There were too many unshared secrets. Too many questions about Michaelis that his parents wanted answers to and he was unwilling to give.

Perhaps Irini was hoping that Sara could exert her feminine influence on Michaelis and get him to open up a little. Perhaps reveal what dark secret was torturing him. Much as she would like to do this, Sara knew it wasn't in her nature to pry.

The sun was slanting over the water, casting a mysterious light over the whole of the bay as Michaelis steered the boat towards the narrow space between the cliffs that led out to the open sea. She looked at him now, standing at the back of the boat, one foot on the tiller as he negotiated the turning point. A wave was coming towards the side of the boat. Michaelis steered towards it and rode over it with the ease of someone whose family had long been used to the unpredictable moods of the sea.

It was a small boat, but capable of a good speed. She leaned back against the woodwork and took deep breaths of the salty sea air. It was chilly out here on the exposed sea, even though Michaelis was hugging the coast. The last rays of the sun were disappearing behind the hill. She watched, stunned by its beauty, as the sun disappeared amid a blaze of orange and red daggers of light that rent the sky before seemingly vanishing into outer space.

Michaelis couldn't leave his place, so Sara moved along the wooden seat to be nearer to him. She hunched down inside his sweater. He'd insisted she put it back on as soon as they'd left the house.

There was a companionable silence, broken only by the sound of the boat's engine and the swishing of the waves against the side. Michaelis seemed deep in thought as he looked out across the water.

Michaelis anticipated a high-swelling wave caused by a large ship further out to sea and turned the boat to take it head on. The little boat cut through the swell with barely a splash. As he wiped some drops of sea water from his face he was wondering what his parents had made of his brief visit this evening. Would it have eased some of their doubts about him? Would it have taken away some of the pain he knew they felt because he refused to confide in them?

They were nearing the turning point into the bay of Nymborio. He sat down on the seat at the back of the boat and, one hand on the tiller, steered the boat carefully around the corner.

Sara moved closer to Michaelis. He smiled and put his arm around her shoulders.

'Not too cold?'

She shook her head. 'I'm still warm inside from the Metaxa. How about you?'

Michaelis laughed. 'I'm always warm.' He hesitated. 'I've enjoyed being with you, Sara.'

'It's been a great day. Thank you for everything. Perhaps we…?'

'Yes?' He pulled her closer.

'Perhaps we could do this again, some time, Michaelis?'

He smiled his mysterious smile. 'Yes, why not?'

She couldn't believe how forward she was becoming! Was it desperation that was driving her to spell it out to Michaelis? Because she wanted to get rid of whatever it was that was holding him back? She'd felt that he wanted to be friends, but beyond that she had no idea what his plans were. She only knew that she wanted a full-blown relationship with this mysterious, infinitely attractive man.

The boat was nearing the jetty in front of their house. So this was no time for pussyfooting around! She took a deep breath.

'Would you like to come in for a drink, Michaelis? Come for supper. My parents will—'

She broke off. Mustn't sound too desperate! That would be a sure-fire way of turning him off.

'I have to get the boat back, Sara,' Michaelis said. 'My father needs it to take him round into Ceres town this evening. He goes everywhere in it. When he was a boy on the island there were no cars, no metalled roads. He still disapproves of the new roads and refuses to use them.'

He cut the engine and leapt on to the shore, holding the thick rope with one hand while he held out the other for Sara.

As she took his hand he drew her against him, bringing his lips swiftly down against her mouth. The impact of his sensual lips took her breath away. She brought her hands up around his neck, pulling his head down towards her so that she could savour the intimate moment more deeply.

And it was only a moment. Michaelis drew himself away as swiftly as he'd initiated the embrace. He waved his hand as he leapt into the boat and started the engine immediately.

She watched from the shore, waving as he steered

the boat out towards the sea again. He gave her a final wave as the boat rounded the corner.

She gave a deep sigh as she climbed up the path that led to the house. She'd hoped this day would never end. She'd wanted to go back to Michaelis's own house, that solitary white building up on the hill. She'd hoped so much that they could be alone together. Really alone.

But for some unknown reason she sensed that Michaelis was fighting shy of such a situation. Why, why, *why?*

She tried to compose herself as she climbed up the stairs to the terrace. Her family mustn't know how her whole life had changed in one day. They wouldn't understand. She didn't understand it herself. It had just happened and she had no idea how she was going to handle her turbulent emotions when she had to work with Michaelis again in hospital.

## CHAPTER FOUR

SARA put down the tray she was carrying and glanced out of the window of the large multi-purpose reception area on the ground floor of the hospital. It was a day similar to the one when she and Michaelis had taken themselves off over the hills. But the weather was definitely much warmer now. Well, they were already in April and the winter weather had given way to spring. She'd hoped that Michaelis would have asked her out again by now, but she'd been disappointed.

He'd been charming and polite whenever they'd met in hospital, but there had been no hint that their day together had meant anything to him. She'd told herself that it probably hadn't been significant to Michaelis. Perhaps he hadn't been as emotionally moved as she had. Probably she'd been just another in the long line of adoring females who vied with each other to go out with their heart-throb medical director. In the short time she'd been working here she'd noticed the expressions of adoration on the faces of the unattached girls in hospital—and some of the attached ones as well!

'Sara!'

'Yes. Sorry, Eleni!' Sara picked up her tray and scurried over to where Eleni was standing beside her desk.

Oh, dear, she hadn't daydreamed like this since she was a student nurse, with a crush on a consultant surgeon who'd unfortunately turned out to be married and therefore untouchable in her code of rules. Michaelis wasn't married, but he might just as well be! His mysterious past was always there as an obstacle between them.

'Would you set up an examination trolley for a renal patient, please? She's due here in a few minutes.'

'Yes, of course.'

Sara hurried over to the treatment room to gather together the equipment she might need for a patient with kidney problems, making a deliberate effort to give one hundred per cent to the task. It had been a quiet morning so far, but now she had to stop her futile daydreaming and concentrate.

It occurred to her that she should have asked more questions about what kind of kidney problems the patient had, but Eleni was now in her office in deep consultation with a visiting doctor from Rhodes and had made it quite clear she didn't wish to be disturbed.

Kidneys were extremely complex organs, Sara thought as she put a packet of sterile swabs on to the trolley. Was this a first-time visit, an emergency, or a follow-up examination? In the multi-purpose function of this unique reception area all things were possible. There was no set working formula for any medical examination.

'Where's the patient, Sara?'

Sara turned quickly at the welcome sound of Michaelis's voice. He was standing just inside the treatment room, sporting that heart-rending smile that always managed to tip her off balance at the wrong time.

She drew in her breath as she tried to steady her nerves and regain her composure.

'I've no idea, Michaelis…I mean, er, Doctor…'

Michaelis smiled. 'Oh, forget the protocol, Sara.' He moved quickly across the room. 'I'm here to talk to a patient with a kidney problem. Eleni tells me she's asked specifically to speak to the medical director, so I think that must be me.'

Michaelis was standing oh, so close to her. The faint scent of his aftershave was sending her emotions into turmoil again. Keep concentrating, girl, and you won't lose your grip, she told herself firmly.

'Eleni asked me to set a trolley for a renal examination but I'm not sure what you'll require.'

'We shan't need any of that,' Michaelis said quietly, motioning towards the array of instruments she'd neatly laid out in preparation. 'As far as I can gather from the notes, our patient has been given all the necessary kidney function tests over in Rhodes, at the hospital renal dialysis unit where she's been having treatment for kidney failure. She's recently arrived on the island and she can manage her own renal dialysis at home. Apparently, she's anxious to talk to me about her prognosis. I've got all the test results here in the notes and—'

He broke off as a small, thin young woman arrived at the door to the treatment room, looking around her with a lost expression.

'Ariadne?' Michaelis enquired gently.

The woman's haunted expression cleared and she gave a slow, uncertain smile. 'That's me. I'm here to see the medical director.'

Michaelis smiled, holding out his hand as if to reassure the highly nervous patient.

'I'm Dr Michaelis Stangos, the medical director. And this is Staff Nurse Sara Metcalfe. We'll go along to my office, where it will be quieter.'

As soon as they were all seated in Michaelis's office, Ariadne wasted no time in explaining the purpose of her visit, occasionally glancing at Sara as if for reassurance.

'As you probably know, Doctor, I've been having renal dialysis three times a week on Rhodes, but since I married a couple of months ago and moved out to Ceres I've been able to do my own dialysis at home. I go to Rhodes once a month for check-ups but...' Ariadne paused, glancing from one to the other of them. 'I'd somehow imagined it would be easier not having to do so many hospital visits...but it's actually harder.'

Michaelis leaned forward across his desk. 'In what way, Ariadne?'

As the young woman fumbled for a tissue in her bag, Sara reached out and touched her hand.

'It's OK to be frank with Dr Stangos,' Sara said reassuringly. 'He's here to help you.'

Ariadne flashed Sara a grateful smile before continuing in a quiet, huskily emotional voice. 'Things aren't going well in my marriage. You see Petros, my new husband, whose family live here, insisted we come and make our home here on Ceres. I wanted to stay in our little house on Rhodes, but Petros said he wouldn't be able to look after me if I got any worse...which I suppose I will.'

'Not necessarily, Ariadne,' Michaelis said gently. 'You're on the transplant list and we're always hopeful that a compatible kidney will become available.'

'Yes, but meanwhile I've got to go on living in

Petros's family's house—the house where he was born. I'm completely under his mother's thumb. I hate it! We've got our own room, of course, but that's the only privacy we have. That's where I have my dialysis treatment.'

'Ariadne, I can't interfere with your living arrangements,' Michaelis said slowly. 'What exactly was it that you thought I could do?'

Ariadne took a deep breath. 'I want you to tell me how long I'm going to have to put up with this waiting for a transplant. I feel like some sort of freak, disappearing to our room for hours on end, and I'm often so tired I simply don't want to join in with the rest of the family when I've finished my treatment. I know I've got kidney failure at the moment, but isn't there something else besides a transplant that could cure me?'

Michaelis glanced down at the notes before replying in a compassionate voice. 'Ariadne, I don't know how much the doctors on Rhodes have explained, but your problem isn't one that will go away. The disease you have is called Berger's disease. It also has a long, unpronounceable medical name which we won't bother with.'

Ariadne nodded and leaned forward, intent on listening to every word the kind doctor was saying.

'I remember that was what the doctor on Rhodes told me, but what exactly is Berger's disease?'

'It's a malfunction of the kidneys caused by the deposit of a substance called IgA antigen. This is normally found in the blood and the inner lining of your intestines, but in your case, and in the case of so many kidney failure patients, the antigen is deposited in the filtering units of the kidney, causing chronic long-term scarring and loss of filtering function. That's why you need the kidney dialysis...'

Michaelis paused before continuing, to make sure Ariadne was following his explanation. 'In the long term, we hope to find a suitable donor for a kidney transplant.'

Ariadne nodded. 'The hospital in Rhodes put me on the transplant list a year ago, but I haven't heard anything. They even said they would airlift me off the island during the winter if a suitable donor turned up, but that hasn't happened. I just want to feel...to be normal again...'

Sara reached for a tissue from the box on Michaelis's desk and handed it to Ariadne, putting her arm around the thin shoulders as her patient's voice became more and more indistinct before petering out in a succession of heart-rending sobs.

'Your life will never be the same as it was,' Sara said gently. 'But if a transplant kidney can be found...'

'They've told me I'm a rare tissue type,' Ariadne said quietly. 'They've asked me to get in touch with my close relatives and ask them to be tested for compatibility. The trouble is, my father and his parents are all dead. My father was an only child, like me, and my mother...well, my mother wouldn't want to help me.'

Michaelis frowned. 'Why not, Ariadne? Your mother surely would be an ideal person to help. Have you asked her?'

Ariadne shook her head. 'I know what the answer would be. You see, my mother abandoned me when I was small. She left my father to bring me up and she went back to Australia, where she was born, back to her boyfriend. My father told me she was a wicked, uncaring mother and I've had no contact with her ever since. So, you see, I haven't got any close relatives.'

She leaned forward, stretching out her hand pleadingly towards Michaelis. 'That's why I came here today, to beg you to exert your influence and try to make my case a priority on the transplant list. I'll do anything that—'

'Ariadne, as soon as a suitable kidney is found you will be taken over to Rhodes immediately. But no amount of pressure on the authorities can make any difference to the fact that you have a rare tissue type and therefore finding a perfect match will take longer. But in the meanwhile…'

Michaelis leaned back against his chair, his face thoughtful. 'You weren't born on Rhodes, were you, Ariadne?'

Ariadne hesitated before answering. 'No, I was born here, on Ceres. That's one of the reasons I didn't want to come back. My dad told me he was so ashamed of the way my mother had behaved he had to get away. It was such a scandal on the island. I mean, a mother leaving her baby to go away with another man!'

'No reason why you should feel ashamed, Ariadne,' Sara said gently. 'You were a perfectly innocent little baby. And these things happen. We don't know all the facts. You mustn't judge your mother by what your father told you.'

'Oh, but I do! That's all he ever said when he told me about the island where I was born. I came to hate the place before I'd even got here.'

'I think you'll find us more hospitable than you

imagined,' Michaelis said carefully. 'Strangely enough…'

He hesitated, knowing it wasn't the least bit strange that he should remember the scandal caused by Ariadne's mother. When he'd looked at her age—twenty-two—in the case notes, he hadn't connected her with the scandal that had once been the talk of the island. He'd been an impressionable sixteen-year-old at the time, and he remembered how shocked he'd been that a mother could walk out on her child. But when he'd heard all the facts…

'Strangely enough, I remember hearing about what happened to you when you were just twelve months old.'

'There! I told you how scandalised people were. No wonder my poor dad had to leave.'

'Most people kept an open mind,' Michaelis said. 'Including me. But it's your present situation that we're talking about.'

He took a deep breath. 'Ariadne, you have to make contact with your mother. She's your best hope of—'

'No. I can't forgive her for what she did. I can't!'

Sara leaned forward and took hold of Ariadne's hand again. 'Sometimes we have to forgive,' she said earnestly. 'You can't go on bearing a grudge against your mother. She brought you into this world. She cradled you in her arms, she fed you, she loved you…'

'Then why did she leave me?' Ariadne raised her tearful eyes and stared at the ceiling, biting her lip. 'What sort of mother can walk out on a twelve-month-old baby?'

'As I recall,' Michaelis said, gently, 'your mother wanted to take you with her, but your father's parents wouldn't let her. She was very young and she didn't know how to fight to keep you.'

Ariadne grabbed a tissue and, leaning back against her chair, started dabbing at her eyes.

'I didn't know that,' she said quietly. 'My father didn't tell me.'

Michaelis remained silent. As he watched Ariadne regaining her composure he was dredging his memory for further clues. From what he could remember of the case, he was sure there was a chance that Ariadne's mother might respond to a plea for help.

'Would you like one of us to get in touch with your mother, Ariadne?' Michaelis said. 'I'm sure if Staff Nurse Sara were to make a phone call and explain she was from the hospital your mother might be persuaded to help you.'

Sara looked enquiringly at Michaelis, but didn't ask any questions at this stage. Negotiations with this highly volatile patient were extremely delicate, and no doubt Michaelis had his reasons for electing her to be the one who made contact.

'If Sara phoned your mother she might get a favourable response,' Michaelis continued. 'It would be a woman-to-woman discussion—and, believe me, Sara is very warm-hearted. If anybody can get through to your mother—'

'Yes, I think I'd like that,' Ariadne broke in. 'You see, I'm absolutely desperate now. Some days, I feel so ill I just want to…to put an end to it all. So I'm definitely not the one to phone up my…my mother. And I think Sara stands a better chance than—'

'A better chance than me,' interrupted Michaelis, in a light-hearted tone. 'Me, a mere man, with a strong Greek accent.'

Ariadne gave a smile as she turned to look at Sara. 'Well, there is that as well. Will you give it a try, then?'

Sara smiled back. 'Of course I will. I'll let you know how I get on as soon as I can.'

'We can't promise we'll be successful,' Michaelis said in a totally professional voice. 'But I think there's a good chance that your mother will want to be tested for compatibility. She would be able to have that done in an Australian hospital.'

Ariadne stood up. 'I hope so. I'd better get back and face the music. Petros thinks I'm shopping down in the town.'

One hand on the back of her chair, she turned to say goodbye. 'Thanks for being so understanding, both of you. I feel a lot easier in my mind now. At least I know there's a chance.'

Michaelis stood up. 'There's also a chance that we mightn't succeed. There are so many considerations, but we'll give it our best shot.'

Ariadne nodded. 'I understand that. I'm prepared now for…for whatever happens. It's good to know I'm not alone in all this.'

'We're here to help you,' Sara said, guiding their patient towards the door.

'Sorry for dropping you in it, Sara,' Michaelis said, coming round the desk as the door closed behind Ariadne. 'You seemed the obvious choice. You're such a natural when a sympathetic manner is required.'

Sara looked up at Michaelis and smiled. 'Is that my main asset? A sympathetic manner?'

'That's only one of your assets. If I told you everything else you'd become too big-headed to contemplate what I have in mind,' he replied in a bantering tone.

Sara had no idea what Michaelis was talking about, but her pulse quickened at the expectant expression on his face.

'And what did you have in mind?'

'A wild evening in a noisy taverna.'

Sara laughed. 'For someone who's just put forward the idea of a wild evening in a taverna you're looking very solemn, Michaelis.'

He gave her a broad grin. 'That's why I proposed it. I've been feeling much too solemn recently. I've been working too hard...we've both been working too hard...and I haven't seen you except in hospital. Where do you spend your evenings, Sara?'

'Usually with my family. If I've been on duty during the evening there isn't much time before I start falling asleep. But tonight you're in luck. I'm off duty from five o'clock, so you can show me the bright lights of Ceres.'

Sara had kept her tone deliberately light. She'd longed for Michaelis to ask her out again, but she'd recognised that for some reason of his own he was reluctant to do that. But now, having spent some time with her in what had been a difficult situation, he'd probably been reminded that they'd enjoyed being together on their day out last month.

And she meant to strike while the iron was hot! If she allowed Michaelis to think too much about this wild evening idea there was a possibility he might change his mind!

'Tonight?' Michaelis queried.

'Yes. Is that a problem?'

She spoke with a firm confidence she didn't feel.

She was putting on an act, playing out of character, but she had to! She wasn't harbouring any hopes that their relationship would move on any further when they were out together, but at least she would spend a few hours with Michaelis in an off duty situation. And that was as far as her sights were set at the moment.

'It's not a problem,' Michaelis said, recovering his composure. 'I'll arrange to be free. Come and meet me here in the office as soon as you can.'

Sara smoothed her hands over her white uniform dress. 'I really ought to go home first to change. I came out in the boat early with Manolis, and I was wearing my old jeans and a sweater.'

'Jeans will be perfect for a night out in Ceres! Phone home and tell Manolis you don't need him to pick you up this evening.'

'OK... Talking of phoning, Michaelis, how do you propose to get the phone number of Ariadne's mother? Australia is a big country and...'

'Trust me, Sara. I'll have the number by tomorrow. Australia might be big, but Ceres is very small. When Sara's mother came out to Ceres as a teenager she used to work in one of the tavernas—actually, the one I'm intending we visit tonight, strangely enough,' he added with a wry grin.

'I see. So we're mixing work with pleasure, are we?' Sara laughed. 'And I thought you were simply taking me out on the town for a wild night out.'

'Do you mind?'

'No, I don't mind at all. I was only joking. I'm as anxious as you are to track down Ariadne's mother. But do you think after all these years...? How many years is it since all this happened?'

'Twenty-one years, to be exact, but I know that Anna, the woman who now owns the taverna, is the same age as Ariadne's mother and they've kept in touch. In fact Anna has been out to Australia to visit her.'

'But how do you know all this?'

'Like I said, everybody knows everybody on this island, and gossiping is one of the main pastimes in the tavernas and cafés. Coupled with the fact that I'm exactly the same age as Ariadne's mother and Anna. We were all just sixteen when this scandal broke and, although most people sided with Ariadne's father, there was a lot of sympathy for the sixteen-year-old mother, trapped in her marriage to an older man and a long way from her homeland. I could tell you a lot more, but...'

The phone was ringing. Michaelis reached over to his desk.

'Yes, Eleni. Sara is still with me. We had a long session with our patient and Sara was most helpful. I couldn't have managed without her.'

Still holding the phone in one hand, he turned to smile at Sara.

'Always the flatterer!' she whispered under her breath as she watched Michaelis listening in to Eleni.

'Would you like to speak to Sara? OK, I'll give her the message right away.'

Michaelis cut the connection and came back towards Sara. 'Eleni has asked if you'll go up to the surgical floor for the rest of the day. One of the staff nurses has had to go home because of a family crisis and they're short-staffed. I suppose you've found out by now that the surgical floor deals with orthopaedics, surgery, obstetrics and gynaecology? Your sister Chloe runs it very efficiently.'

Sara smiled. 'It will give me a chance to catch up with her. We're often on different duties, and I'm usually down in the reception area, so I've only worked with Chloe a couple of times.'

She turned and began to move towards the door. Michaelis moved with her, putting his hands on her shoulders to keep her a while longer.

'Thanks for your help this morning.' He leaned forward and kissed the side of her cheek.

It was only a friendly peck, and didn't merit the rush of excitement that Sara felt. She looked up into those dark brown eyes but Michaelis was giving no indication of his feelings.

'Do you kiss all your staff as they're leaving?' she asked lightly, giving him a flirtatious smile.

His expression changed. He looked suddenly vulnerable and apprehensive as he drew her against him, bringing his lips down on hers.

She savoured his ardent kiss. This more than made up for the perfunctory peck on the cheek. She could feel her body becoming liquid with desire and she longed to give in to the sensual excitement she felt. But even as the wild thought came into her head she knew she had to draw back. This was no place to follow her heart.

Gently, she pulled herself away from Michaelis's embrace, looking up into his eyes searchingly.

He cupped her face with his hands. 'Tonight?' he said.

The unanswered question hung in the air. Was Michaelis making a suggestion that they continue where they'd just left off? Was there a hint that their relationship could be about to take off?

'Tonight,' Sara replied quietly.

Michaelis leaned against the closed door, listening to the sound of Sara's receding footsteps in the corridor.

He'd almost let himself get carried away just now. For three whole weeks he'd been oh, so careful when he encountered Sara in hospital. He'd been at his most professional during the times they'd had to work together. But today…!

He walked over to the window and gazed down at the boats bobbing in the harbour. He raised his eyes up to the windmills near where they'd had their picnic on that idyllic day. Sara had affected him so profoundly then that he'd known he had to be on his guard. Sara, more than anyone he'd ever met—even his wife in their early heady days when everything was going well between them—seemed as if she could become his soul mate. He felt as if he'd known her all his life.

He turned away and went back to his desk. Sitting down, he tried to tell himself that he'd got to get a grip. He was in danger of falling in love. Whatever that meant he had no idea. He just knew he was consumed with a deep attraction towards Sara and he wanted to go further. Just now, he'd only intended to give her a chaste kiss. But when his lips had touched that soft, fragrant skin…

He drew in his breath as he recognised that he wanted so desperately to make love with Sara. But that was exactly what it would be…making love. There was no way he could have a simply sexual encounter with Sara. It would be all or nothing. His emotions would be totally involved. He would find himself completely enslaved by her. And then…

What if she went on to break his heart—his heart which was still bleeding from the last time? Could he cope a second time?

# CHAPTER FIVE

SARA tapped on Michaelis's door. It was opened almost immediately by Panayota, his secretary.

'Dr Michaelis has been called away to the medical floor, but he asked if you would wait for him here, Sara.'

Panayota held open the door to allow Sara in.

'Would you like some coffee while you're waiting?'

Sara smiled and said she would. 'Black, please.'

Panayota poured a cup from the tray on Michaelis's desk holding a cafetière and two cups, before handing it to Sara with a smile.

'I have to go home now, Sara, but I don't think our medical director will be long.'

Sara recognised that the very smart Panayota was scrutinising her appearance and she wished she hadn't changed back into her old jeans. She felt much more confident and less vulnerable in her uniform.

As the door closed behind Panayota Sara looked around her. It was only hours since she'd left here and she couldn't help wondering if Michaelis was regretting that ardent, wonderful…

She drew in her breath as she remembered the touch of his lips, the way his hands had caressed her. It had been so difficult to get back into working mode. She was sure that Chloe had suspected something when she'd reported to her for duty on the surgical floor. Twice Chloe had asked if she was feeling all right: once when she'd dropped a kidney dish of used disposable instruments on to the floor and another time when she'd started putting a counterpane, instead of a sheet, directly on to a patient's mattress.

'Ah, you've made it!' Michaelis breezed in through the door. 'How was your time on the surgical floor with your big sister? Did Sister Chloe make you work too hard?'

'She never stopped cracking the whip. And I didn't have to phone Manolis to cancel the boat because Chloe needs a lift home tonight. She's promised to explain to Mum and Dad why I'll be late.'

Michaelis poured himself a cup of coffee and sat down on the nearside of the desk beside Sara.

'Do you think they'll approve?' he asked lightly.

Sara grinned. 'You mean will they approve of me going out with the distinguished medical director of Ceres hospital?'

She found it necessary to joke. Their passionate kiss this morning had put a new dimension on their relationship. She suspected that they were both tense, both watching to see if they'd overstepped the mark. Neither of them knew if it was what the other one wanted. And neither of them wanted to make the first move towards recapturing that heady feeling they'd experienced only hours before.

Michaelis smiled. 'I meant will they approve of Michaelis the man taking their precious youngest daughter out on the town?'

'I may be the youngest, but at twenty-seven I've been around… Oh, I don't mean—'

'I know what you mean, Sara. You've done a lot of living. You must tell me about it some time. But now…'

He was standing up and taking her cup from her hands. 'Now it's time to escape this establishment—make our getaway. First, a drink on the harbour will relax us, I think.'

Sara certainly hoped it would! They needed something to break the ice this evening.

Michaelis parked the car in a narrow little side street, deftly manoeuvring it between a small, disused rowing boat and a pile of wicker baskets, with the remains of this morning's catch giving off a pungent odour.

'We'll have a drink on the harbourside,' Michaelis said, guiding Sara out of the narrow street towards the wider paving area near the sea, 'and then I'll take you to Chorio, the upper town, where Anna has her taverna. She's a superb cook, so that's where we'll have supper.'

'And get that important phone number,' Sara prompted quietly.

'Don't worry, I haven't forgotten. That's one of the purposes of our visit...and the other is to enjoy ourselves,' Michaelis added hastily, a mischievous grin on his face.

With his hand on the small of Sara's back he drew her towards a taverna beside the water.

'We'll sit outside and watch the boats in the harbour. It's always amusing to watch the tourists dressing up for a night on the town. The people who tie up their expensive yachts here don't know it's best to dress down in the evening.'

Sara laughed as she glanced down at her old jeans. 'I'm glad about that.'

A young Greek waiter came out of the taverna and stopped beside their table.

'What would you like to drink, Sara?' Michaelis asked.

'Have an ouzo on the house,' the waiter suggested, giving Sara a broad smile that revealed brilliant white teeth in his dark face. 'Your first time here, isn't it? The first drink is always free.'

The young waiter's carefree *joie de vivre* broke through Sara's reticence. She smiled. 'Why not? An ouzo would be just the drink for me tonight.'

'And for you, Dr Michaelis?'

'I'll have an ouzo, too.'

The waiter went inside. The string of fairy lights hanging at the front of the taverna were illuminated at the same time as the haunting Greek music started from somewhere inside the taverna.

The drinks were brought to the table. Michaelis poured water from the small jug into their drinks. Sara watched, fascinated, as the ouzo turned cloudy.

'Here's to our evening out on Ceres!' Michaelis said, clinking his glass against Sara's.

As she sipped her drink, Sara could feel herself relaxing. Glancing at Michaelis, she saw that strange, faraway expression in his eyes, as if he was reliving some memorable experience.

She pointed across the harbour to the opposite hill-side. 'Look, you can see the sun shining on the top of our windmills.'

Michaelis's expression changed. 'Our windmills,' he repeated softly. 'I like that, Sara.' He put his hand across the table and took hold of Sara's. 'I like your child-like enthusiasm for life.'

Sara was puzzled. 'Is that meant to be a compliment?'

'It's just a statement of how I see you,' he said, his

voice husky with emotion. 'I remember I was attracted by your lively enthusiasm on that first evening when I met you at your family home in England.'

'I didn't know that,' Sara said, feeling deliciously calm as the soothing touch of Michaelis's fingers made shivers run up her arm. 'But you were married.'

'And you were only sixteen,' Michaelis said, with mock solemnity. 'And I was definitely put off by the way you made fun of my accent.'

'I wasn't making fun. My sisters and I always used to get terrible attacks of the giggles when we were supposed to be polite to a guest. And what you said about my spots…'

Michaelis burst out laughing. 'Oh, please, don't bring that up again.' He squeezed her hand. 'Drink up and I'll take you out for supper, just so long as you don't make fun of my accent.'

'Only if you don't mention my spots!'

'What spots? You never had spots, did you, Sara…?'

Michaelis held on to her hand as they walked along the harbourside. She was glad they were back in easy-going mood. A friendly rapport was all she hoped for this evening. On the other hand, if romance began to blossom…

They sat on the outside terrace of Anna's taverna. Below them, looking over the rooftops of the hillside houses, Sara could see the harbour. Beyond that was the sea, and far in the distance the Turkish mountains, dimly covered in an evening haze, dark purple and orange in colour.

On the hair-raising drive up the zigzagging road that led to the taverna Sara had held her breath at each corner. Once they'd had to pull over to allow the island bus to pass by on the other side of the road. Michaelis, having driven that way many times, had taken everything in his stride, but Sara had been glad when they reached the safety of the taverna.

A plump Greek woman of indeterminate age, probably fortyish, Sara decided, was approaching them from the inside of the taverna. She smiled broadly when she saw Michaelis.

'*Kalispera,* Michaelis!'

'*Kalispera.* Good evening, Anna. This is Sara, the new staff nurse at our hospital.'

'Welcome, Sara! What will you have to drink? Ouzo? The first drink is on the house.'

'Yes, please.' Sara smiled.

'Is the first drink always on the house?' she asked Michaelis as Anna disappeared inside through the beribboned curtain.

Michaelis nodded. 'Usually it is. Especially for friends and regulars who live on Ceres.'

'I'd better take a lot of water with this one,' Sara said, as the drinks appeared.

Michaelis looked up at Anna as she hovered by their table. 'Have you time to have a drink with us, Anna? There's something I want to discuss with you.'

'I can always make time for a drink with friends.' Anna hurried inside and returned with a glass of ouzo for herself.

'Anna and I were at primary school together,' Michaelis said as he pulled up another chair at their table for Anna.

Anna smiled. Until that moment Sara had thought she looked much older than Michaelis. But a smile could take years off a person's face. She seemed to lose the middle-aged impression she'd given when they first arrived, and Michaelis had said she was his own age—thirty-seven.

'And now I have four children,' Anna said. 'A great blessing, but a lot of hard work!'

Michaelis nodded. 'A great blessing,' he repeated softly.

Sara, watching the sad expression on his face, saw that Anna was also looking anxiously at Michaelis. It was obvious that Michaelis had hoped for a family of his own, but the premature death of his wife had ended those hopes.

'What did you want to talk to me about, Michaelis?'

'Your Australian friend. I've forgotten her name, but you know who I mean. I believe you went out to stay with her again last year? You took your two younger children with you for a holiday?'

Anna looked startled. 'You mean Sylvia?'

'Yes, that's her name. She got married and had a baby here on the island, and—'

'Yes, yes, we don't need to drag all that up again.'

Michaelis put down his glass. 'I'm afraid we do. You see, Sylvia's daughter has been in touch with me and—'

'No, don't tell me any more! Sylvia has been trying to forget the baby she had on Ceres ever since they took her away from her. She's never got over the way she was treated and I've agreed never to speak about the baby she lost. Sylvia has her own life now. She and Don got married after her divorce came through, and they've got three wonderful children, so…'

Her voice trailed away as she saw the pleading expression in Michaelis's eyes.

'Anna, it's a matter of life or death,' he said quietly. 'Ariadne, Sylvia's daughter, needs a kidney transplant. Sylvia is her only hope.'

Anna leaned back against her chair, a look of anguish on her face. 'I'm really sorry. I can't speak for Sylvia but I think it will bring it all back—how Vasilis and his parents turned her out of the house when they knew she'd been phoning Don in Australia, and...'

'But don't you think Sylvia will want to save her daughter's life?'

Anna looked troubled. 'As a mother, I know she would. I know I'd do anything for my kids... Tell you what, I don't want to be the one to upset her, but I'll give you Sylvia's phone number and you can phone her if you really think there's no other way.'

Michaelis's pleading expression changed to one of relief. 'Thanks, Anna. Actually, Sara will probably make the phone call. I think Sylvia is more likely to listen to another woman than me.'

Anna gave a slow smile. 'You were counting on me giving you that number, weren't you?'

Michaelis returned her smile. 'I knew I could count on you, Anna. I could always rely on you to give me some of your sweets in the playground at playtime.'

Anna burst out laughing. 'Only because I fancied you. You were always the best-looking boy in the school.' She clapped a hand over her mouth as she began giggling girlishly. 'Mustn't let my husband hear me saying that.'

Anna stood up and hurried away inside, to emerge, seconds later, with her diary. 'Here it is. Sylvia Greenwood—she's married to Don Greenwood.'

Quickly Anna scribbled down the number on a paper napkin and handed it to Michaelis, who put it in his pocket.

'Don't ring tonight,' Anna said. 'They're eight hours ahead of Greek time, so they'll all be asleep. Try them in the morning. Now, are you staying for supper? Yes? OK, come in the kitchen and see what I've made today. There's lamb stew or lamb *souvlakia*—that's kebabs roasted on a skewer over charcoal,' she explained to Sara, who was following her inside.

The delicious smell of the food from the oven was tantalising Sara's nostrils. The kitchen was warm and cosy. A couple of young girls were stacking plates and wiping glasses.

'My daughters give me a hand in the evening when they've finished their school work,' Anna said as she began opening the oven door and bringing out large casseroles. 'There's *stifado*—that's a beef casserole. It tastes good with some of my *gigantes*—those are large beans. You'll find they…'

Sara listened fascinated as the array of dishes was explained. Every dish that Anna produced seemed like the one she would prefer, only for her to change her mind when something else was displayed.

She looked up at Michaelis. 'It all looks so delicious. What would you recommend?'

'Anna does a superb *mezze*,' Michaelis said. 'That way we get to try lots of dishes.'

Anna smiled approvingly. 'Good idea, Michaelis.'

'Just keep the dishes coming, Anna. We'll take our time. We've got all night.'

And the dishes did keep coming! Sara tried to pace herself by tasting small amounts of each succulent dish. They began with *dolmades*—stuffed vine leaves—followed by two kinds of fish, together with prawns and crab in the starter course. Then, moving on to meat dishes, Sara could have tasted lamb, beef and chicken, but decided to restrict herself to chicken so that she would have room for the *gigantes*, aubergines and artichokes.

Michaelis topped up her glass with wine as she put down her fork and leaned back against her chair, declaring that she couldn't eat another morsel.

'That was superb!'

Michaelis smiled. 'The food is always excellent here. Anna's father started a good family tradition of first-class cooking in this taverna. When he died three years ago Anna took over from him, and standards have actually improved. I often come here for supper.'

'Don't you ever cook for yourself at home?'

A haunted expression crossed Michaelis's handsome face. 'Why would I want to do that? It's no fun eating by yourself.'

'So you're not a real recluse, living up there on the hillside all by yourself, are you?'

'I've chosen to live alone because…because it's easier that way. No complications, no commitments…'

His voice trailed away.

'So, have you given up on commitment, Michaelis?'

'That depends,' he said quietly.

He leaned back in his chair as he reflected that the pain was always there. The heart-breaking pain of disillusion. He couldn't go through all that again! But would he have to with someone like Sara? Someone who seemed so utterly trustworthy?

But that was how Krysanthe had seemed until… He forced himself not to dwell on the unpleasant details. He didn't want to change the light-hearted mood he was trying to create for this evening.

Sara would be different. He had to take a chance. He couldn't go on regretting the past for the rest of his life. Sara had encouraged him to believe she was attracted to him. All the signs were that he wouldn't be rejected if he was to follow his heart.

Slowly, he leaned across the table and took hold of Sara's hand.

'Let's go back to my reclusive house,' he murmured. 'At least I can make coffee. I'd like you to see where I live all by myself…that's unless you prefer to have coffee here.'

'I'd love to see your house.'

Michaelis was standing up now, coming round, holding the back of her chair. She remembered the way he'd said, 'Tonight,' as he'd held her in his arms at the hospital this morning. That hint of a magical promise. Perhaps tonight really was going to be special.

She hoped so! She had absolutely no reservations now about moving on in her relationship with Michaelis. The more she was with him, the more she learned about him, the more she wanted him. As she walked with Michaelis to the door she was aware of the touch of his hand under her arm. Why was this man so different from anyone she'd ever met?

She'd had other boyfriends who'd interested her for a short time. When she was twenty, she remembered, Steven had been fun to be with. And then, a couple of years ago, her short affair with David had seemed promising—only to fizzle out when they'd both decided they didn't have enough in common to stay together in a lasting relationship. And there had been no spark, no fire. There'd been no real depth in David. Nothing to intrigue her the way Michaelis did. Nobody had ever excited her the way Michaelis did now. He carried around him an aura of virile intensity which gave out a powerful magnetic force that simply drew her towards him and made her want to be with him for…well, for ever!

But for ever was asking too much. She'd settle for this evening to begin with. Possibly longer if…

Michaelis was helping her to climb up into the sturdy Land Rover. It was a large step up from the ground and she really needed help. She wasn't just feigning helplessness to bring out Michaelis's gallant nature, even though she enjoyed the experience of feeling his arms around her as he lifted her up into her seat!

She strapped herself in. The seat belt buckle needed adjusting. She'd meant to do it when they left the harbour. Michaelis leaned across and tightened the strap for her. One hand on her waist, he drew her towards him. His lips were gentle as he kissed her. She felt a surge of sensual anticipation.

Perhaps this really was going to be a very special night. She wasn't going to hold back. She felt as if she really was getting through to Michaelis, helping to convince him to leave the past behind him and move on.

But nothing was ever certain where love was concerned. Yes, she'd fallen in love with Michaelis, but she had no idea how he felt about her. They'd shared tender romantic moments together, but Sara didn't dare to hope for anything more than that. Michaelis was his own man and would decide if she was worth giving up his self-imposed solitude.

Sara watched Michaelis now as he drove away from the taverna, his jaw firmly set as he concentrated on the winding road that led through the upper town. Did he have any idea how much she wanted him tonight? She knew, from various snippets of information she'd gleaned from Chloe and some of her friends, that Michaelis had a reputation for being something of a Don Juan figure. Many a girl on the island had vied to become his special girlfriend. But nobody had succeeded. Brief flings were all he'd allowed himself since the death of his wife.

She stifled the sigh that rose to her lips as she leaned back against the leather seat. What made her think she was going to be any different? What made her believe she was the one who was going to change Michaelis?

No, she shouldn't try to change him. She didn't want to change anything about him. She would enjoy a brief romance, if that was all their friendship turned into. And then she would try to forget him.

Her eyes were moist as she looked out through the windscreen at the dark road ahead, lit only by their headlights. A goat, temporarily blinded by the bright lights, stood in the middle of the road, its staring red eyes mesmerised by the pool of frightening illumination.

Michaelis slammed on the brakes and came to a halt with only inches to spare. The goat gave a hoarse cry before scrambling over the wall at the side of the road and disappearing back up the hillside.

Michaelis ran a hand through his dark hair. 'That was a close shave! I'm always on the look-out for animals when I come home along this road. The goats aren't used to seeing vehicles along here, and they regard the road as an extension of the hillside, part of their own territory.'

'Is it your own private road?'

Michaelis nodded as he restarted the engine. 'I'll have to do something about the cracks in the surface soon. We had a lot of rain in the winter and parts of the road turned into a rushing stream. But there'll be plenty of time to get some workmen on to it during the summer, when we have very little rain.'

Michaelis remained silent for the rest of the drive. They were climbing higher up the hill now, and then, in the headlights, Sara caught her first close-up glimpse of Michaelis's house. She'd seen it from a distance when she was at his parents' house on the other side of the valley. Close up, she could appreciate just how big and impressive it was.

'Don't you find yourself rattling around in such a huge house?' she asked as Michaelis switched off the engine.

'Rattling around? What is that?'

'Sorry! It's a silly expression. I meant to say the house looks too big for just one person.'

'I didn't even notice when I bought it.' Michaelis jumped down and came round to help her from the car. 'I just needed a place to live on my own and this had been on the market for ages so it was going cheap.'

Still holding her hands, he looked down at her. Only the moon was illuminating his features now. Sara shivered.

'You're cold, Sara. Let's get you inside.'

He put an arm around her as he guided her inside. The warmth of the sun had been trapped inside the house all day and a welcoming cosiness wrapped around her as she went in through the unlocked door.

'Don't you lock up when you leave your house?'

'No need to lock doors out here. I know everybody who might come up and they're all honest. There's a woman from the village who comes once a week to clean through the house and do the laundry, but apart from that…'

Michaelis spread his hands wide. 'It's the perfect place to come back to after a hard day's work at the hospital. I usually sit out here on the terrace.'

He led the way through long plate-glass windows on to a rather grand crazy-paved area with views over the valley and, far below, the bay, with lights from the moored boats twinkling on the dark water.

She sat down beside him on a small wicker sofa, leaning back against the squashy feather cushions.

'I'll make the coffee in a few minutes,' he said, putting his arm around her shoulders and drawing her against his side.

Sara smiled. 'No hurry. I like sitting here admiring this wonderful view. It's so peaceful up here on the hillside. I can see why you love it.'

'It was a spur-of-the-moment decision when I bought it. I'd just lost Krysanthe. My world was falling apart. It was at the end of a long evening with friends in a taverna down in Ceres harbour. Everybody had been telling me what I should do with my life and I said I simply wanted to get away and live by myself for a while.'

Michaelis's fingers tightened on her shoulders as if he was reliving that evening.

'I remember there was a man from Athens playing cards at the next table. He leaned across and said he had a house for sale that would suit me. He'd been renovating this old place as a holiday home which he'd planned to rent out to tourists. He'd run out of money and he wanted to go home to Athens as soon as possible. He couldn't finish the project so he said he'd sell it cheap.'

'And you agreed? Without seeing it?'

'Oh, I knew where it was. I used to play up here when I was a child. It was an old ruin and my friends and I used to run in and out of it, climbing the rickety old stairs. There had been a lot of talk about how this stranger to Ceres had spent a lot of money on the renovation. So when he named his price I snapped it up. It needed lots doing to it…still does…'

Michaelis waved a hand towards the wooden roof of the terrace where patches of damp could be seen.

'But I'm getting there. You wait till you see the bedrooms…'

He broke off, a rakish grin on his face. 'Gave myself away then, didn't I?'

Sara smiled up into his eyes. 'I wasn't under any illusions when I came here tonight. I hoped you were going to show me round the house, and perhaps…just perhaps…'

Michaelis stood up and drew Sara to her feet. She leaned against him, revelling in the strong, muscular feel of his body.

'Sara,' he murmured, holding her so closely that she felt as if she had already melted inside him. 'Are you sure?' he whispered, his eyes scanning her face.

She nodded. 'If we don't make love tonight…'

Michaelis was already scooping her up in his arms…

Sara lay back on the white sheet and looked up at Michaelis. She'd barely registered the climb up the stairs, the hurried discarding of their clothes. Her body felt as if it was on fire as she tried to drown herself in the tender expression in Michaelis's eyes.

His fingers, gently caressing her body, were driving her wild with longing. She wanted to prolong the wonder of their lovemaking but she knew that she couldn't hold out much longer against her desire for the ultimate fulfilment.

'Yes, oh, yes!' she breathed as Michaelis entered her.

It seemed so right to be absorbed into each other. This was what she'd been searching for all her life. The feeling of belonging to her soul mate.

The rhythm of their lovemaking became more frenzied, both of them striving to please the other, both of them hurtling towards that final climax that would bring them heavenly release from their erotic tension.

Sara cried out in ecstasy again and again as they climaxed together, clinging to Michaelis as if she would never let him go. She was no longer in the real world. She'd flown away to some heavenly planet, far away above the clouds, where only the two of them would live for ever…

The pale light of dawn was creeping into the room. Sara opened her eyes and experienced a feeling of unreality creeping over her. She'd stayed all night with Michaelis. All those hours, when they'd turned to each other and made love repeatedly—sometimes hurriedly, sometimes with a languid somnolence that had turned Sara's body into liquid fire.

Michaelis, lying beside her, one arm flung above his head, looked as calm and innocent as a child. His face was relaxed in sleep, his sensual mouth curved in a smile. She felt a surge of love towards him.

She'd committed herself to this wonderful man over and over again during the night. But how would Michaelis feel about their lovemaking when he woke up and cold reality set in? This meant so much to her. Michaelis had seemed so ardently in love with her. It couldn't have been simply an act…could it? It must have meant something to him…or perhaps it hadn't. Perhaps he was such a skilful lover he could convince someone that they were the only person in the world for him when in reality…

Michaelis stirred, as if sensing Sara was watching him. Languidly he reached out and drew her against him. As she snuggled closer she longed to ask questions. So many thoughts were running through her mind, but she didn't dare spoil the delicious ambience that enveloped them. Besides, she could feel the stirring of desire deep down inside her once more, and with his renewed caresses Michaelis was leaving her in no doubt about how he felt at that moment…

It was the blazing of the sun through the open window that woke her. She glanced at the clock.

'Look at the time! Wake up, Michaelis!'

He opened his eyes and stretched out his arms towards her.

'No, Michaelis. I'm on duty in half an hour.'

He grinned. 'And you think the medical director will notice if you're late?'

'No, but Chloe will. She wasn't all that convinced this was a good idea when I phoned from Anna's taverna to say I would be late. I'd better phone home now. They'll have noticed I didn't get back last night.'

He cupped her face in his hands. 'Don't worry. As you said yourself, you're old enough to lead your own life.'

He kissed her briefly on the lips before she got out of bed and made for the door leading to the bathroom. Grabbing a towelling robe from the hook, she peeped round the bedroom door again.

'I'd rather hoped there would be time to make that phone call to Sylvia in Australia before I went into hospital.'

'You can phone from my office as soon as we get in.'

She went back into the bathroom, closing the door, and made her way over to the shower cubicle.

'Yes, it would be a good idea for me to be in your office, Michaelis.' She raised her voice but didn't know if Michaelis could hear her. 'I need to be sitting down, all calm and collected. I don't know when I've felt so scared about making a phone call before.'

When she climbed out of the shower she glanced around her at the huge bathroom. It was a very opulent room, no expense spared in the gold fitments and ornate carvings on the walls and roof. This was one part of the house that had been well finished off before the previous owner's money ran out. Or maybe Michaelis had instigated this section after he'd moved in.

If only she'd had more time she would have luxuriated in that divine bath. Definitely designed as a two-person bath! Her mind raced ahead to the possibilities. Not today, but if she was invited back…

Padding back into the bedroom wearing the huge towelling robe, she almost collided with Michaelis. He'd tied a towel round his waist and she felt a renewed stirring of desire as he drew her towards him. Even the cascading of the shower hadn't dampened the tingling feeling in her skin. She would have loved to return to bed and spend the rest of the day there.

'Got to go!' she said quickly, making a determined effort to escape his embrace.

Michaelis gave a deep sigh. 'I suppose we have to make a start. OK, I'll get you to my office in double-quick time. And now, if you're sure you've finished with my bathrobe, Staff Nurse…'

Sara laughed as Michaelis pretended to reach, playfully, for the belt of the robe. He grinned before turning away and striding barefoot into the bathroom.

Pulling on her jeans and sweater as she listened to the sound of Michaelis's shower, Sara had no idea how she was ever going to come down to earth again! The night she'd just spent with Michaelis had changed her for ever. She was utterly enslaved—and that wasn't always a good state to be in when you couldn't vouch that the other person felt the same way. Not that she'd ever been in this position before. Enslavement was something about which she had absolutely no experience.

Meanwhile, there was work to be done at the hospital. She had to get her head together and try to act in a normal way, even though nothing would ever be the same again.

## CHAPTER SIX

WAS it really only yesterday evening that she'd sat in this chair waiting for Michaelis to arrive? It seemed like a lifetime ago! A lifetime of change. The hours spent making love with Michaelis had changed her for ever. She would never be the same again. Whatever transpired in their relationship in the future, she would always hold on to the memory of the wonderful night she'd spent in Michaelis's arms.

She looked across the desk at him now. He was checking out the contents of the first letter on the top of his pile, frowning at something he was reading and making a note on the scribble pad beside him.

'Do you need any help, Dr Michaelis?' Panayota put her head round the door that led into her office. 'I'm free to type up the answers to your letters as soon as you've prepared them.'

'We'll do that later, Panayota. Sara is going to make an important phone call, so we don't wish to be disturbed for the next few minutes.'

'More coffee?'

'No, thank you, Panayota.'

Sara breathed a sigh of relief as the secretary retreated into her room. She'd felt even more vulnerable than usual this morning when she'd arrived in Michaelis's office and downed her first cup of coffee. The sensual rapport between herself and Michaelis must have been so blatantly obvious.

She opened the case notes in front of her, scanning

as much as she would need to know to answer any questions that Ariadne's mother might ask over the phone.

All supposing Mrs Sylvia Greenwood was at home. If she wasn't at home then Sara would have to leave a message, but that would be so unsatisfactory. Sara knew she couldn't possibly disclose the nature of her call to the rest of the family. It was possible that Sylvia's children didn't know they had a half-sister. Perhaps…

'You're nervous, aren't you, Sara?'

Michaelis put down the letter he'd been pretending to read and reached for Sara's hand across the desk. 'I'm truly grateful that you're making this call for me. But if you really feel you can't go through with it…'

'Of course I can do it! If you'll dial the number now, I'll get on with it.'

Michaelis gave Sara a reassuring smile as he consulted the number written on the paper napkin that Anna had given him on the previous evening.

It was ringing. All those miles away in Australia, where it would now be late afternoon, early evening. Sara reviewed the first sentence she planned to say to Sylvia and…

'Hello?' A female voice answered, bright, welcoming.

She was in luck! 'Is that Mrs Sylvia Greenwood?'

'Sorry, dear. You've just missed her. I'm Fiona Greenwood—Don's mother. Can I help you?'

Ah, Sylvia's mother-in-law. How much did she know about Sylvia's previous marriage and the abandoned baby? Sara knew she definitely mustn't divulge any details that Sylvia might have kept secret.

'I'd prefer to speak to Sylvia. Can you tell me when she'll be back?'

'Now, that I couldn't say. Sylvia and Don have gone off on holiday in their camper van for a few weeks. First time they've been away without the kids. That's why I'm here to look after them. Well, they're all at school during the day, so it's not difficult. What did you say your name was, dear?'

'I'm Sara Metcalfe…a friend of Anna—the lady who stays with Sylvia sometimes.'

'Yes, I've met Anna. But you don't sound Greek.'

'I'm English.' Sara glanced across the desk at Michaelis, who had pushed a note towards her.

*Don't explain about the kidney,* Michaelis had written.

'I'll call again when Sylvia returns,' Sara said.

'Yes, that would be best. In a few weeks she'll be back. Maybe before if they start missing the kids—which is unlikely!'

Sara felt a pang of dismay as she mentally reviewed the state of Ariadne's health. Her dialysis treatment was keeping her health stable at the moment, but if the kidney failure grew any worse…

'Is there anywhere I could get in touch with Sylvia in the meantime?'

'You could leave messages at the campsites they've planned to visit when they're travelling, but I've promised only to do that in an emergency. They haven't even taken their mobile phone. It's their wedding anniversary and they want a complete break on their own. Isn't that romantic?'

'Yes, they sound like a happy couple.'

'Oh, they are. I couldn't ask for a better daughter-in-law. Sure you don't want to tell me…?'

'I'll call back in a couple of weeks,' Sara said quickly.

'Yes, you do that, dear. Bye!'

Sara looked across the desk at Michaelis. 'Oh, it's so frustrating! Sylvia Greenwood and her husband are away for "a few weeks", whatever that means. Sylvia has a charming mother-in-law, heart of gold, but she sounded terribly vague. I'll call in a couple of weeks and see if there's any news. If not I'll just keep on phoning till I finally contact her.'

'Ariadne's in no danger at the moment,' Michaelis told her reassuringly. 'She's lucky to be given this chance. But it is only a chance. You were quite right not to give out any information about why you were phoning. We don't want Sylvia's family to become alarmed. It would be a major upheaval in their lives if Sylvia agreed to donate a kidney.'

Sara leaned back against her chair. 'Sylvia's tissue type may not even be compatible with Ariadne's. Genetics is a very complicated subject, and it does sometimes happen that mother and daughter tissue types aren't compatible. Even if they are, Sylvia may simply refuse.'

Michaelis came round the desk and drew Sara to her feet. 'We mustn't get despondent,' he said quietly. 'We have to keep on hoping.'

Sara looked up into his eyes and revelled in the deep sympathy of his expression. He was such a caring, compassionate doctor and she loved him very much.

'In the meantime we'll have to keep Ariadne's spirits up,' she said.

Michaelis nodded. 'I'll talk to her this morning.

You may speak better English, but my Greek is better than yours,' he added with a wry smile.

The phone was ringing. Michaelis reached across the desk. 'Yes, Eleni? Sara is with me here. She was making an important phone call for me... Of course...'

Sara smiled. 'Don't tell me... I'm on my way there now...'

'You're needed in reception as soon as possible. An accident on the new road, Eleni said. You're to assist Andonis in the plaster room. I understand you're quite an expert in setting broken bones.'

Sara paused by the door. 'Well, it's not difficult,' she said, shrugging self-deprecatingly. 'I did a course in plaster techniques at the end of my nursing training and it's been very useful here. There's always somebody falling and fracturing a limb on this island.'

'Only the goats know how to fall without hurting themselves,' Michaelis said, moving towards her. 'You wait till the summer tourists arrive. You'll wish you hadn't shown how skilful you were in the plaster room.'

Sara gave a mock groan. 'I'd better go.'

Michaelis put a finger under her chin, tilting her face towards him. 'Thanks, Sara,' he said huskily.

She drew in her breath. She didn't know whether he was referring to the phone call or their shared experience of the last few hours. But all good things came to an end. She had to come down to earth.

Smoothing down the skirt of her uniform, and making a determined effort to gather her thoughts and become professional again, she hurried away.

Andonis was one of Sara's favourite doctors to work with in the hospital. She'd enjoyed meeting him on that first evening when he'd come to the house for the dinner party. His knowledge of orthopaedics was considerable and she always felt confident when he made a diagnosis.

She found him now, studying the X-rays of a young man who was lying on the examination couch.

'Ah, there you are, Sara. I asked Eleni if you could help me. I haven't called you away from anything urgent, have I?'

'No, I was just coming.' Sara smiled down at the patient. 'So, what happened to you?'

The young Englishman pulled a wry face. 'It's only my second day out here, Nurse. I hired a motorbike yesterday and drove miles over all sorts of rough tracks without any problem. Today, I'm simply minding my own business, driving up that winding road from the harbour, and…smack, bang, wham! I skidded on the corner, went straight into the side of this dirty big lorry, and next thing I know, I'm on the road… Not a good place to be with a hangover like mine!'

'So, you overindulged last night, did you?'

The young man grinned. 'You could say that. Well, first night on holiday—you know what it's like. Well, maybe you don't, but anyway, my name's Tom.'

The patient tried to move his arm and gave a loud groan. 'Ouch! Put my hand out to save myself and that was it. Could have been worse. Might have been my leg.'

'Excuse me a moment, Tom,' Sara said, moving across the room to examine the X-rays.

'Is this the only injury, Dr Andonis?'

The doctor nodded. 'Tom's been very lucky. Just

this fracture here in the radius. It's a clean break, so five or six weeks in plaster should be sufficient. We won't even need to manipulate it. I'll hold the arm in the correct position while you put the plaster on.'

Andonis explained to their patient the treatment he was going to receive. The young man said he was relieved it wasn't more serious.

'That's a smart-looking plaster you're using,' Tom said, as Sara prepared to encase his arm.

'Yes, it's a special kind of splint. It's made from multiple layers of a knitted fibreglass fabric, impregnated with polyurethane resin. It's covered on one side by an air- and moisture-permeable non-woven fabric, and on the other side by fast-drying air- and moisture-permeable open-cell foam, which serves as padding.'

'Wow! It certainly beats the old plaster they put on me when I was a kid and broke my leg falling out of a tree. Weighed a ton, that one did.'

'Yes, you'll find this one is much lighter, even though it's very strong,' Sara said as she removed the splint from its foil pouch.

Carefully, she immersed the splint in water, before squeezing it a couple of times while it was still submerged. Removing it from the water, she squeezed out the excess liquid and blotted the foam side on its absorbent surface.

With Andonis holding Tom's arm in position, Sara applied the splint with the foam side against the skin.

'The splint's going hard now, isn't it, Nurse?' Tom remarked as he looked down at his arm to see what was happening.

Sara nodded. 'Yes, exposure of the splint to water initiates a chemical reaction which causes the splint to become rigid. I'm now going to encase the splint in an elastic bandage at the same time as I'm moulding and forming it with my hands. See how it moulds exactly to your arm, holding it in the correct position?'

Tom nodded. 'It's not as painful now.'

'That's partly the painkillers I gave you,' Andonis said. 'But the arm will certainly feel more comfortable now that Sara has set it in position. I'd like to keep you in for a few hours. If you're feeling OK at the end of the afternoon we'll discharge you, but for the moment I'd like you to rest on the orthopaedic ward. I'll come and see you after lunch. Could you take Tom up there, Sara? Tell Chloe it's for observation purposes only. It's all in the notes. Tom fainted at the scene of the accident but I don't think he was concussed.'

'Hungover, I was, Doctor,' Tom said. 'Everything went fuzzy. I didn't exactly black out. But I wouldn't mind a kip on a bed so long as one of these nice nurses is going to look after me.'

'Ah, the wanderer returns,' Chloe said quietly as Sara arrived on the surgical floor, walking beside the porter who was pushing Tom's wheelchair.

Sara handed over her patient's notes. 'I'll explain later,' she whispered, before raising her voice so that Tom could hear what she was saying. 'Meanwhile, Andonis has requested you observe our patient. He fainted at the scene of his accident, apparently, and we're being extra cautious because of his fragile condition, due to a hangover.'

Her patient grinned. 'Should have stayed in bed today.'

'Will you see our patient into that bed over there in the alcove, Staff Nurse?' Chloe asked, in a professional tone. 'And then perhaps you might have time for a word before you go back to Reception. I'll be in my office.'

Sara made sure that Tom was comfortable.

'Would you like a cup of tea or coffee?' she asked him.

'I'd rather have a beer, Nurse! You know—hair of the dog?'

Sara gave her patient a wry smile as she poured out a glass of water. 'Drink a few glasses of water and it will help to rehydrate you, Tom.'

She made her way to Chloe's office, which was in a central position on the surgical floor. It was from here that Chloe coped with all the administration of this busy section of the hospital. Sara was impressed by the way her sister managed to hold down this important job and still have plenty of energy left for her children when she got home.

'Coffee, Sara?' Chloe asked, picking up the large cafetière on her desk.

'Yes, please. I thought you'd brought me in here to give me a dressing down. Was Mum annoyed I didn't get in last night?'

'Not annoyed, exactly. You're not a child. And she never tried to discipline us even when we were young, did she? But she looked a bit worried. She knew you were with Michaelis and…well, I think she might know something we don't know about him.'

Sara felt as if a chill wind had blown over her. 'What do you mean, Chloe?'

'Oh, since the death of Michaelis's wife there have always been rumours and conjecture about how she died, apparently. Mum didn't say much, but I gather she's worried you might get hurt.'

'Get hurt? In what way?'

'Oh, not physically, I don't suppose,' Chloe said quickly. 'Emotionally, perhaps? I'm not sure it's a good idea to become too fond of Michaelis. He doesn't easily make lasting friendships any more. And he doesn't discuss his private life. Nobody really knows what happened when his wife died.'

Sara was stunned by the revelation. 'Where did she die?'

'In the hospital, but—'

'Well, then, why all the mystery? The hospital records will have all the details.'

'Michaelis brought his wife in, but it was too late to save her. Krisanthe had been alone when she miscarried their child.'

'She was alone when she miscarried?' Sara echoed incredulously. 'But where was Michaelis?'

'I don't know,' Chloe said in a firm tone. 'And I don't think we should discuss this any more here in the hospital.' She leaned forward and put her hand on her sister's arm. 'Look, don't worry. I know you'll be sensible and won't let yourself get carried away where Michaelis is concerned.'

Sara swallowed hard. It was too late! She was already hopelessly in love. But this was, after all, only rumour. Michaelis must have had a good reason for not being with his wife when she went into labour. But what an awful thing to happen! No wonder Michaelis didn't want to talk about his tragic marriage.

'I thought I'd find you here, Sara!'

She looked up, startled by the sound of Michaelis's

voice. The door to Chloe's office was open and he was standing on the threshold. Sara felt a flush rising to her cheeks as she tried to banish her thoughts. She felt guilty at harbouring the vague doubts that Chloe had implanted in her mind.

'Do come in, Michaelis,' Chloe said, at her most professional, as ever, when a medical colleague arrived. 'I'll go and get on with my work if you've simply come to see Sara.'

'I've come to see Sara about a patient we're dealing with, Chloe.'

'Then I'll leave you to your discussion,' Chloe said in clipped tones, and she walked quickly towards the door.

'Oh, dear, I think I've upset your sister,' Michaelis said.

Sara had recovered her composure. 'Don't worry. She's not too pleased with me this morning.'

'Ah, staying out all night, I suppose?' Michaelis moved closer.

'Something like that.'

Sara felt herself coming under Michaelis's spell once more as he put his hands on her shoulders and looked down into her eyes.

'This really is a professional call,' he told her, the enigmatic expression in his eyes giving nothing away. 'I've been speaking to Ariadne on the phone and she'd like to see both of us this afternoon.'

'I'll be there.'

Michaelis's eyes clouded over. 'Is everything OK, Sara? You seem a bit tense.'

'I'm fine!' She put on a bright smile. 'But I ought to get back to Reception and do some work.'

'I'll come with you. I need to see Andonis about his orthopaedic surgical schedules.'

They walked together down the stairs. Side by side with Michaelis, Sara couldn't imagine that the rumours Chloe had spoken of could be anything but wild conjecture. From what she'd seen of Michaelis he was the kindest, most considerate man. He wouldn't hurt a fly.

But as she looked up at him now, when they reached the bottom step, she gave a shiver of apprehension. There were areas in Michaelis's life she knew nothing about. She only had her gut feeling to rely on. And still wearing the rose-coloured spectacles that coloured her ideas of his character didn't help in making an objective judgement.

'Ah, Andonis,' Michaelis said, stretching out his hand towards their colleague. 'Just the man I wanted to see…'

'I'll go and report to Eleni,' Sara said quickly.

Their meeting with Ariadne went well that afternoon. To allay their patient's fears Michaelis gave Ariadne the latest results of her kidney function tests and a full physical examination, checking her out and assuring her that there had been no further deterioration in her kidneys. Her dialysis routine was proving effective.

'So it's just a question of waiting until you can speak to my mother?' Ariadne said as Michaelis and Sara walked with her to the office door.

'Yes, we'll let you know as soon as we've been able to make contact with her,' Sara said, smiling at her patient as she said goodbye.

Ariadne was their last patient of the day. It was

already after the time that Sara was supposed to go off duty and she was feeling particularly tired.

'So, would you like a drink on the harbour?' Michaelis asked.

Sara smiled up at him. 'That's what you said yesterday evening.'

Michaelis gave her a rakish grin. 'And look what happened after that. I'm not suggesting a long evening, simply a drink and then perhaps…'

'I ought to get back home,' Sara said. 'I'm in the doghouse as it is.'

'The doghouse?'

Sara laughed. 'Sorry—another silly expression. I need to have an early night. I've been particularly tired today.'

'Me too,' he said, his voice husky, tantalisingly sexy.

Sara felt a shiver of excitement running down her spine as he drew her into the circle of his arms. She raised her face to his and savoured their long, lingering kiss.

'I must go,' she whispered. 'I don't want to keep Chloe and Manolis waiting for me.'

'So, are you going to go home and be the dutiful daughter tonight?' he whispered, his hands beginning to caress her slowly, arousing her dormant senses once more.

Gently she pulled herself away, before she changed her mind and succumbed to the thought of another night of ecstatic pleasure.

'I must go,' she said, with a determination that was hard to maintain.

With a sigh he released her completely from his

arms and stood looking down at her with a resigned expression.

'Well, make sure you're free of your family commitments at the weekend. It's Easter and the whole of Ceres will be celebrating.'

'I'll look forward to that,' she said, tearing herself away as her resolution began to falter.

Changing from her uniform back into jeans and sweater in the tiny changing area, Sara told herself that she wouldn't dwell on any of the remarks that her sister had made about Michaelis. She was going to keep an open mind. She wasn't going to listen to rumours that had been bandied about from person to person until they'd grown out of all proportion to fact and become pure speculative fiction. Maybe one day, when she'd really gained Michaelis's trust, he might decide to tell her the secret about his past.

She wasn't going to pry...but oh, loving him as she did, it was so hard to keep silent.

She hurried down to the harbour. Manolis and Chloe were waiting for her. Manolis immediately started the engine as she went aboard.

'Hope I haven't kept you waiting.'

'I've only been here a few minutes,' Chloe said, as the boat sped out across the water. 'I gathered that you'd been held up.'

Sara nodded, studiously keeping her eyes on the water ahead. She wasn't going to be drawn into any more discussions about Michaelis. She was going to think positively. She wasn't going to think about these flimsy rumours.

But it was difficult to discard them totally. There was no smoke without fire, her father always said.

She shivered as a chill wind blew in from the open sea. She was determined to give Michaelis the benefit of the doubt. She loved him so much now that she couldn't bear to think about what she would do if Michaelis wasn't as totally honest as she'd imagined.

## CHAPTER SEVEN

IT WAS Easter Sunday before Sara was able to escape from her family commitments. There had been dinner parties on both Friday and Saturday evenings, when she'd been expected to help her mother and sister. Since coming out to the island to live her parents had gathered a large group of friends amongst the Greek and English people with homes on Ceres. Consequently, their social diary was always full.

Sara had sensed that her mother would be disappointed if she said she'd made other plans for those evenings. And so, as both evenings dragged slowly along, her thoughts had turned constantly to wondering what Michaelis was doing. Sara told herself that it was no bad thing to have a period when they didn't see each other. The veiled, nebulous suspicions that Chloe had planted in her mind were decidedly upsetting, and she needed time to sort out her feelings.

Now, as Manolis steered the boat round the corner towards Ceres town, she felt relieved to be getting away at last. Her family were staying behind in Nymborio. She'd been told that the harbour would be impossibly crowded on Easter Sunday morning. But she didn't mind, just so long as she was able to find the taverna where she'd promised to meet Michaelis…and there he was!

She stood up in the boat and waved. Suddenly feeling that Manolis didn't entirely approve of her childish display she sat down again. But Michaelis had already seen her, and with his studied, languid stride he strolled over to the harbourside.

There was no place in the crowded harbour where Manolis could tie up the boat. Every available berth had been taken. As Sara waited, Manolis tossed Michaelis the thick, knotted rope. Michaelis hauled the boat in towards the harbourside, into a narrow gap between two larger boats, holding it in position long enough for Sara to jump out on to the quay.

'What time shall I come back for you, Sara?' Manolis asked.

'I'll bring Sara home,' Michaelis intervened quickly as he took hold of her hand.

Sara hesitated. 'Don't you think it would be more sensible if I arrange a time for Manolis to be here, Michaelis?' she said.

Michaelis grinned. 'Yes, it would be more sensible, but it will be more fun if I take you home.'

He waved a dismissive hand towards Manolis as he led Sara away from the waterside towards the taverna where he'd been sitting.

'Now, sit down here at this table, Sara, and take that solemn look off your face. Waiter!' he called, and he snapped his fingers.

Their drinks arrived in double-quick time. Michaelis leaned forward and took hold of her hand again. 'I've missed you, Sara.'

Her heart missed a beat as she looked up into his eyes. 'I've missed you too.'

Sara glanced around her. People were looking in their direction. Feeling decidedly conspicuous, she removed her hand from Michaelis's grasp and leaned back against her chair.

'Tell me what's going to happen here, Michaelis,' she said quickly.

He smiled. 'The Easter procession's just started. The procession will come along the harbourside, led by the band. See the drummer over there? And they've got some fine trumpets this year.'

Sara smiled back at Michaelis. 'So I can hear.' She had to raise her voice above the sound of the loud music that was drawing closer as the procession moved slowly towards them.

'And then there'll be dancing over there by the clock tower,' Michaelis said, pointing along the harbour. 'After that there will be fireworks and—'

'More fireworks!' Sara said. 'The fireworks haven't stopped since Friday. All I could hear throughout the night was explosive sounds echoing round the hills.'

'Oh, the young men always go up into the hills to set off the really noisy fireworks. Some of them are literally dynamite. Trouble is there are usually one or two young men who take too many risks, and that's when the accidents happen. I've only scheduled a skeleton staff to be at the hospital over Easter. Everybody wants to be off duty. But I'm on call for emergencies, along with several other members of staff.'

'That's reassuring!'

Michaelis smiled. 'Reassuring, but it could interrupt our day. I gave you the entire weekend off because you had family commitments. How did it go, all the socialising?'

'Oh…it was a bit of a strain. I'm glad to be here today.'

Sara didn't want to elaborate. She had no desire to discuss her family with Michaelis. She wanted to forget the way her mother and sister had looked at her with worried expressions on their faces as she'd set off this morning to meet Michaelis.

A shadow fell across their table. Sara shielded her eyes from the sun and gave a start of recognition.

'*Yassoo,* Stavros—hello.'

Sara hadn't seen her musically inclined acquaintance since the night he'd come to her first dinner party soon after she'd arrived on Ceres, but he had the sort of distinctive face you didn't forget in a hurry. Heavily bearded, with dark bushy eyebrows, his face was a forest of hair and it was difficult to decide what he would look like if he shaved it all off.

'Hope I'm not interrupting anything,' Stavros said, pulling up a chair and sitting down beside her.

'No, not at all.' Sara smiled warmly.

Glancing at Michaelis, she saw that the expression on his face was one of open hostility. She could feel the tension rising as both men studiously ignored the other.

'I wanted to ask if you could help me to organise the Ceres music festival, Sara,' Stavros said earnestly, watching the reaction on her face. 'It's not until August, but we need all the helpers we can get, and you, with your excellent musical background—'

'Sara will be too busy at the hospital,' Michaelis interrupted in an ominous voice. 'I couldn't possibly allow her to take time off.'

'Oh, I wasn't suggesting Sara take time off,' Stavros said nervously before Sara could speak. 'This would all be in Sara's free time. And, if I may say so, I think it's for Sara to decide what she does in her off duty.'

Stavros turned to look at Sara, his eyes pleading

for her to give him a little time to explain. 'I've written a musical for the children of the island. It's based on the story of Ceres and Proserpine and I know the children will love performing it.'

In spite of the unfavourable situation Sara found herself in, she knew she wanted to help with this musical project.

'Stavros, I'll have to think about this,' Sara said in a placatory tone. 'If you could let me know exactly how you would want me to help I could—'

Michaelis was already standing up, taking Sara's hand firmly in his. 'Sara, you would be making a big mistake to get involved. Goodbye, Stavros.'

Sara was about to object to Michaelis's behaviour but Stavros nodded. 'I'll send you a copy of the musical score, Sara, and give you some more details when…'

Stavros's voice was drowned in the noise of the approaching procession. The drums and trumpets were passing nearby. Children and adults dressed in colourful traditional Greek costumes were walking behind the band, waving to their friends, their faces wreathed in smiles, so happy and proud to be taking part in the Easter Sunday procession.

'The procession always signifies the start of spring,' Michaelis told Sara, raising his voice above the loud music of the band as he led her along a narrow street towards another taverna. 'We shall be quieter here,' he said, holding out a chair for Sara to sit down.

'Michaelis, don't you think it was rather rude of us to walk away from Stavros like that?' she said quietly, as she pulled her chair closer to the table.

Michaelis frowned. 'Rude? What do you mean?

We hadn't invited that man to sit at our table.' His voice rose angrily. 'He had no right to presume that he could interrupt us like that. Stavros was the one who was rude.'

'Michaelis, he is supposed to be a friend. He's offered to let me play his piano and—'

'No!' Michaelis frowned heavily. 'You mustn't go to his house, Sara. You mustn't! Promise me—'

He broke off, sensing that he'd almost said too much. He mustn't, he couldn't reveal the truth. He'd promised…

Sara reached across the table and covered his large hand with her own in a sympathetic gesture as she saw the anguish on his face.

'What is it, Michaelis? What grudge do you have against Stavros? As far as I can see—'

'Sara, you know nothing about that man…but I can't explain why you mustn't see him alone. You have to trust me on this.'

So, it was all down to trust again, Sara thought, as she looked across the table. Once more she had to trust Michaelis, and once again she felt confused by the events she was caught up in. She was trapped in a web of conflict. Here, on this idyllic island, just when she'd thought she'd found the love of her life, there were unknown, hostile forces threatening to spoil her relationship with Michaelis.

She honestly felt that Michaelis had overreacted just now. Stavros seemed such a mild-mannered man. Her parents had told her that he was an excellent pianist and singer who'd studied in Athens before making his home on the island. He had some kind of private income which enabled him to devote his time to organising various music events.

She reflected how much she would like to join in those music events in her off duty time. And the offer of being able to play on Stavros's piano was very tempting. It was going to be some time before she could get a piano shipped out here, and she didn't want to waste all those years of her musical training. But how could she go and play Stavros's piano when Michaelis had begged her not to?

She took a sip from the glass of wine which Michaelis had placed in front of her while she considered what she was going to do. Michaelis was being very high-handed with her over this problem. Even though she was hopelessly in love with him, her own sense of independence made her rebel against being told what to do. Unless some concrete evidence against Stavros presented itself she would make her own decision about whether to help with the forthcoming music festival.

She took a deep breath. 'Michaelis, I have to say—'

'Excuse me, Sara.' Michaelis took his mobile phone from his pocket as it began to shrill.

His face was solemn. '*Endaxi.* OK. I'm coming, Eleni.'

Sara looked at Michaelis enquiringly as he stood up. 'What's the problem?'

'That was Eleni at the hospital. A young man has just been brought in with a badly injured hand.'

Sara jumped to her feet. 'I'll come with you.'

'Are you sure? You're not on call, Sara.'

'I'd like to help.'

* * *

Eleni looked up in surprise as Sara arrived with Michaelis. But the expression on her face was welcoming towards both of them.

'Thanks for coming, Michaelis. Are you here to work, Sara?'

'If I'm needed.'

'Oh, you're needed all right!' Eleni smiled gratefully. 'We've had another injury admitted since I phoned you. A little boy with a broken arm.'

'I'll deal with the injured hand first. Perhaps you could phone one of the other doctors on call, Eleni, to examine the little boy?' Michaelis said quickly.

'I'll check the on-call rota. Dr Andonis is available, I believe. This way, Doctor.' Eleni pulled back the curtain around one of the cubicles.

The young man was cradling his heavily bandaged right hand against him. Chattering away in Greek, he explained how he'd been lighting a firework and it had exploded sooner than he'd thought it would.

'His whole hand has been hurt,' said his anxious mother, getting up from her seat beside the examination couch. 'And...'

The mother's voice faltered and a frightened expression crossed her face.

'And what?' Michaelis prompted gently.

'One of his fingers was blown off in the explosion. I've wrapped it up and brought it. It's here in my bag...look, Doctor. Do you think you can...?'

Michaelis took the small package from the patient's mother. Carefully he unwrapped it and examined the contents. He glanced at Sara.

'I think it might be possible to sew this back on to the hand,' Michaelis said quietly. 'I don't think we should attempt it here, because it needs a surgeon who's experienced in this delicate kind of surgery, but there's a surgeon at the hospital in Rhodes who has a high success rate with injuries of this kind.'

'I'll pack the finger in ice until it's needed,' Sara said. 'I had a case almost identical to this in Accident and Emergency in London last November. That's when we set off our fireworks and light bonfires.'

Sara looked more closely at the finger. It didn't appear to be damaged, but re-attaching it to the hand required a very special skill.

'The finger looks viable to me, but, as you say, it requires an expert,' she said quietly.

Michaelis nodded. He had already picked up the phone and was dialling the surgeon's number. As Sara packed ice around the finger she listened to Michaelis making arrangements for their patient to be airlifted to Rhodes by the helicopter ambulance. Placing the precious ice-packed finger in a special container, Sara returned to her patient.

'*Posseleni?* What's your name?' she asked gently.

'Cristiano,' the young man said, in a wavering voice. 'Will you be able to sew my finger back on?'

'There is a clever surgeon on Rhodes who is going to try, Cristiano.'

Michaelis returned and looked anxiously down at their patient. 'You have to understand that the operation might not succeed,' he said. 'We'll do everything we can, but…'

'It's OK, Doctor,' Cristiano's mother put in. 'My son is a courageous boy. He will accept whatever happens. I have to go back to the rest of my family now. I have three younger sons waiting at home to hear what has happened to their big brother. I know you will take care of him, Doctor. Now, be a big strong boy, Cristiano.'

'Of course I will,' Cristiano said, in a firm voice. 'But, Doctor, will you come with me to Rhodes?'

'Yes, I'll come,' Michaelis said. 'Another doctor has just arrived here at the hospital to take my place.'

Andonis came across the reception area, buttoning up his white coat. 'I'm going to take care of the young boy with the broken arm, Michaelis. The ambulance is waiting to take you to the helicopter pad.'

'Thanks, Andonis.' Michaelis looked across at Sara. 'We need a qualified nurse to be on hand for the journey to Rhodes. Eleni has to stay here. I know you're not on call, but would you be able to come with us, Sara?'

'Of course.'

The helicopter was flying low over the water, sometimes almost skimming the waves as it made its way to the island of Rhodes. Sara, sitting beside her patient, glanced out of the window and was surprised to see a couple of dolphins leaping out of the water in a graceful arc of movement. The helicopter climbed higher above the sea and the boats below looked like tiny toys.

Although she was saddened by the plight of her patient, Sara was glad she was able to help in this emergency. It meant more to her to be doing the job she loved on this Easter Sunday than simply be enjoying herself amongst the crowds back there on Ceres. And it was good to be working with Michaelis.

She glanced across at him now and wondered how she could possibly doubt his integrity. Whatever secrets he was guarding, she was sure it couldn't be anything sinister.

Her patient's dark skin was looking unnaturally

pallid. He must be suffering delayed shock. Sara reached for the sphygmomanometer and took Cristiano's blood pressure again. It had fallen slightly since she last took it, but that was understandable in the circumstances. She checked his pulse and temperature. Both were slightly above normal but not dangerously so.

'We'll be at the hospital landing pad in a few minutes,' Michaelis said, bending over their patient. 'How's the pain in your hand now?'

'It's better since you gave me that injection,' Cristiano said. 'I wish you were going to do the operation on me, Dr Michaelis.'

Michaelis smiled. 'I prefer to put you in the capable hands of an expert in this kind of surgery. My colleague will do everything he can for you.'

Cristiano nodded resignedly. 'But will you and Nurse Sara stay with me until they put me to sleep?'

'Of course we will,' Michaelis said, looking at Sara who nodded her assent.

The helicopter was descending now, coming down vertically on to the large letter H, landing with expert precision in the centre of the pad.

The pilot cut the engine and suddenly everything seemed unnaturally quiet after the noise that had been non-stop since they left Ceres. The air outside was calm again now that the huge blades had stopped rotating. Sara could see a porter pushing a trolley towards their helicopter. He was accompanied by a man in a white coat and a nurse.

'Are you ready now, Cristiano?' Sara asked gently.

Her patient nodded. 'I'm OK. But please don't leave me.'

* * *

In the ante-room of the theatre, Sara looked across the motionless form of their patient and smiled at Michaelis.

'He's peaceful now,' she said, feeling a sense of relief that they could leave Cristiano in the expert care of the surgical team who were waiting to begin the operation.

She watched as Cristiano was wheeled into Theatre. The swing doors closed.

'That's our job completed,' Michaelis said. 'The pilot is waiting to take us back to Ceres. We'll be able to phone later to find out how Cristiano is.'

'And how successful the surgeon has been,' Sara said quietly. 'There's nothing more we can do but pray for a successful outcome.'

Suddenly she felt a deep sense of anticlimax. She'd been geared up to take care of her patient and now he was no longer her responsibility. She could feel her eyes misting over. It was difficult to remain totally professional when you became attached to a brave young patient.

'Cristiano has been so brave,' Sara said, her voice husky with emotion. 'You could see he was sad about losing his finger, but he didn't complain or…'

'Come on, Sara,' Michaelis said gently. 'Let's get you home. This wasn't what I'd planned for our Easter Sunday, but thanks for working with me.'

Once she was in the ambulance, a deep weariness came over her. She leaned against Michaelis, whose arm was around her shoulder. He drew her against him, stroking her hair until she felt herself slipping into a state of blissful soporific calm.

* * *

'We're almost back at Ceres, Sara,' Michaelis murmured.

Sara opened her eyes. She'd slept for the entire journey back over the water. Looking out of the window, she could see that the darkened island was bejewelled with a myriad of tiny lights as the helicopter descended from the night sky. As the pilot cut the engines and the doors opened, the first thing Sara heard was the sound of more fireworks echoing across the valley.

Michaelis held her hand as she went down the steps.

'Are you OK, Sara? You look a bit…'

'I'm fine. Just tired, that's all. And worried about the fireworks going off. If only the youngsters setting light to them could see the anguish poor Cristiano has suffered they might think twice about taking risks.'

'Youngsters will always take risks,' Michaelis said, leading her across to the waiting ambulance. 'It's part of growing up. We have to learn by our mistakes. Experience makes you a wiser person in the end.'

She climbed into the ambulance. Michaelis sat down beside her, his arm lightly resting on her shoulders.

'Experience is sometimes hard to take,' Sara said slowly. 'There are some events in my life that I could have done without. How about you?'

Glancing at Michaelis, Sara could see that his eyes held the faraway expression she'd seen so often. As if he was crying inside but keeping up a brave face on the outside.

'There are lots of things I'd like to change in my life.' Michaelis's voice was even. 'When you have no control over something, that's when it hurts the most.'

She felt his fingers tightening on her shoulders and she longed to turn and hold him in her arms. What was this secret that was in danger of coming between them? How could she find out without destroying the precious rapport that was building up between them?

## CHAPTER EIGHT

SARA could feel the strong heat of the sun on her face as Manolis steered the boat towards Ceres town. They were nearing the end of April, but it felt more like the middle of summer.

She thanked Manolis and said she wouldn't need a lift home that evening. Michaelis was going to drive her back later.

Walking up the short road that led to the hospital, she could feel her spirits lifting at the thought of seeing Michaelis again. She'd been late off duty last night, so they hadn't met up after work. How many hours was it since they'd worked in the hospital together? She'd never been in love like this before, and her love for Michaelis coloured everything she did. But her happiness was still marred by the fact that Michaelis hadn't yet confided in her about what was troubling him.

Since the Easter celebrations a couple of weeks ago there had been so many occasions when she'd longed to ask him for the truth about the death of his wife. But she'd remained silent so as not to spoil the fragile rapport that existed between them. She'd seen how Michaelis's moods could change quickly if he was angry about something, and she'd sensed that he was treating her more cautiously since they'd argued over Stavros asking for Sara's help with the music festival.

Going into the hospital, she remembered the dark, angry expression on Michaelis's face when Stavros had joined them at their table on Easter Sunday. She wouldn't dare risk having Michaelis become angry with her if she became inquisitive and tried to pry into his past.

The young girl on the reception counter called across to Sara. 'Dr Michaelis has asked if you would go to his office as soon as you arrive, Staff Nurse.'

Sara felt her heart give a little hop, skip and jump. What a good way to start the day!

Michaelis stood up and came round the desk to greet her. For a moment he held her close, gently kissing her on the cheek, before releasing her from his embrace and looking down into her eyes.

Yes, Sara still held that troubled expression on her face, Michaelis thought anxiously. She'd become more distant with him in the last couple of weeks. It was almost as if she'd sensed his secret and didn't dare trust him any more. Perhaps some of the rumours about his wife had filtered through to her. But he was the only one who knew the truth, and he was sworn to secrecy.

He hadn't dared to ask her back to his house again. There had been so many evenings when she'd made some kind of excuse about having to get back. And even when he'd driven her round the bay to Nymborio and stopped outside her house she hadn't asked him to go inside.

Had he come on too strong during that idyllic night they'd spent together? Perhaps it had been too early in their relationship. Maybe he should have waited longer. But Sara had given him every encouragement. She'd wanted to make love with him. He'd been in no doubt about that at the time. But now he didn't know how he should behave towards her if he wasn't to frighten her away.

He stifled a sigh of frustration as he went back to his desk and tried to concentrate his thoughts on professional matters.

'Come and sit down. Good news about Cristiano. He's back at home on Ceres and the operation to sew back his finger has been successful. The surgeon phoned me last night at home to say all the tests prove that circulation in the hand is normal again. There is slight loss of movement in the finger, but nothing that Cristiano cannot get used to.'

'That's wonderful!'

'It's good to have success with a patient. I wish all our medical ventures were as successful. I keep thinking about Ariadne and hoping we'll find a compatible kidney for her.'

Sara frowned. 'I'll have to try and contact her mother again. I phoned last week, and her mother-in-law said Sylvia is still on holiday with her husband. But she expects them to come home any day now.'

'Would you like to try again this morning?'

Sara nodded. 'No time like the present.'

She sat down and picked up the phone. Michaelis resumed his seat behind the desk.

'It's ringing.' Sara found she was holding her breath, as she always did when she tried to contact the elusive Sylvia.

The Schubert song 'Who is Sylvia?' was going through her head. She began to hum it as she waited for someone to answer.

'It's not "Who is Sylvia?"' she said under her breath as the ringing sound continued unanswered.

'It's Where is Sylvia...? Oh, hello, Mrs Greenwood? Mrs Sylvia Greenwood?'

'Yes, I'm Sylvia Greenwood. Who's speaking, please?'

It was a nice calm voice. A pleasant-sounding, happy voice. Sara swallowed hard. She had to make a success of this first time.

'My name is Sara Metcalfe. I'm a staff nurse at the hospital on Ceres. I've been trying to contact you...'

Sara spoke slowly and carefully. She'd rehearsed what she was going to say so many times, had even found herself waking in the night and explaining how important it was that Sylvia Greenwood should agree to help her daughter. The daughter she hadn't seen since she was a baby. It could be Ariadne's last chance, because with her rare tissue type there was only a slim chance of finding a compatible donor kidney.

Sara put forward all the arguments in favour of Sylvia helping her daughter. At first Sylvia listened in silence. Possibly she was stunned by the revelation that her now grown-up daughter was suffering from chronic kidney failure. Perhaps she was regretting leaving her behind to be brought up by her first husband's family.

'It's very difficult for me, Staff Nurse,' Sylvia said warily.

'Please call me Sara. I hope you'll come to look on me as a friend. And may I call you Sylvia?'

'Of course. Everybody does.' Some of the feisty, good-natured tone returned. 'I know you're only doing your job, but you have to see how difficult it is for me. Only my husband knows I was married and had a child when I lived for that year on Ceres. I deliberately kept it from his mother and I didn't tell my children. I've tried to forget Ariadne myself, but…'

For a few seconds there was silence, broken only by the sound of a rustling tissue.

'You see I was very young—just sixteen. I'd left school, but hadn't a clue what I wanted to do. I was more or less engaged to Don, who's a couple of years older than me, but we had a silly quarrel one day and I broke off our engagement. I didn't really mean it. Thought he'd come running after me, but he didn't. Then I got the idea of going away for a bit—that would teach him. You know how you do with fellas…'

Sara listened as Sylvia's words came out in a rush. She was reliving the past. The young lovers' tiff, taking out all her savings, her impulsive flight to the Greek island, looking for work in a taverna, imagining she was attracted to a much older, more experienced Greek man…

'When I discovered I was pregnant I was horrified,' Sylvia continued.

Sara looked across the desk at Michaelis, who was watching her carefully. His eyes held a questioning expression.

'Everything OK, Sara?' he mouthed silently.

Sara nodded. She felt it was important to be patient with Sylvia. She had to get her story off her chest before there was any chance she might agree to help the daughter she'd abandoned.

'And you were all alone without friends or relatives, weren't you?' Sara prompted gently, trying desperately to gain Sylvia's confidence.

'Exactly, Sara! So, like the young idiot I was, I

turned to the man who'd put me in the club in the first place! Well, I had no money left. I couldn't escape from the island without money, and I knew it would be hard to keep working when my pregnancy became obvious. Vasilis was pleased I was pregnant. He'd always wanted a child. His first wife, who'd died a few years before, hadn't been able to give him children. So he took me home, settled me in his mother's house and we got married.'

Another long pause, then, 'I have never been so miserable in my life. Even before Ariadne was born I started planning to leave, trying to save up a few drachmas here and there when I could get my hands on some, so I could scrape up the money for a ticket back to Australia to find Don again.'

'But what about the baby?'

'Oh, I was going to take the baby with me, of course. But when I told Vasilis's family I was leaving, they refused to let Ariadne go with me. I think they were glad to see the back of me. They practically turned me out when they knew what I planned to do. They gave me enough money to buy my ticket and have something to live on for a while when I got back to Australia. So, although it broke my heart, I had to leave Ariadne behind.'

'Sylvia, I know you loved Ariadne…'

'I still do. I've never stopped thinking about her.'

'Then please help her. Tell me the name of your nearest hospital. I'll send details of the tests we would like you to have to check whether your kidney would be compatible with Ariadne's.'

'But would I be able to manage with only one kidney if I gave Ariadne one of mine?'

'Yes. The human body can function perfectly well

with just one kidney. Lots of people have donated a kidney to a relative and then gone on to lead healthy lives. But the first step is to determine whether you're compatible or not, Sylvia. Will you go to the hospital and take the tests?'

Sara almost jumped for joy when Sylvia agreed to take the first step. She continued to advise Sylvia about what would be required of her, answering all her questions and even giving out her personal phone number so that Sylvia could contact her at any time she felt worried.

'Sylvia's agreed!' Sara's hand still rested on the phone as she looked across the desk at Michaelis.

He smiled broadly. 'So I gathered. Well done! Shall I give Ariadne the good news that her mother is going to take the first step?'

Sara smiled back. 'Yes, phone her now. Though I suppose we shouldn't raise her hopes too much in case…'

'I'll be diplomatic,' Michaelis said.

Sara stood up. 'I ought to go and do some work. I haven't reported to Eleni yet.'

Michaelis stood up and came round the desk. 'We're going to see each other tonight, aren't we?'

Sara nodded happily. Michaelis leaned forward and touched her lips lightly with his own. There was a promise of sensual excitement in his lips. She felt her body tingling with delicious anticipation. Maybe tonight she would be able to forget the doubts she'd harboured since Chloe had tried to disillusion her about Michaelis. She longed for the feel of his arms around her all through the night. Such pleasures shouldn't be denied because of an unsubstantiated rumour.

She looked up into Michaelis's eyes and felt a physical ache surging through her body. Consummating her passion with Michaelis had been the most wonderful experience. Her body had never been so alive, so fulfilled.

'Yes, I want to see you tonight,' she whispered, standing on tiptoe to kiss Michaelis once more, full on the lips.

His arms tightened around her. 'Sara...'

His voice was full of sensual promise, but Sara didn't get to hear what he was going to say. The door from his secretary's room was opening and both of them sprang apart and assumed their professional roles.

Sara walked away, hurrying down the corridor towards the busy reception area to begin her work.

She functioned efficiently throughout the rest of the day, keeping her mind firmly on the medical tasks she was performing. But somewhere at the back of her mind there was the reminder of the evening to come, and the possibility of another idyllic night with Michaelis.

Sara spent a good part of her day in the plaster room. There were more tourists on the island now that the weather had warmed up, and tourists meant more accidents. What was it about holidays that made normal human beings throw caution to the wind and attempt to behave like mountain goats?

As she applied her last plaster of the day to a young woman who'd attempted to climb a crumbly cliff and then put out her hand to save herself as she fell to the ground, Sara was definitely feeling as if she needed a rest.

'Thanks, Staff Nurse,' her patient said, as she ran her uninjured hand tentatively over the still-wet plaster.

'Your plaster will harden up very quickly, so just stay still for a few minutes,' Sara said, pushing back a lock of hair that had fallen over her face as she'd leaned over her patient.

'Still here, Sara?'

Sara smiled as she heard the welcome sound of Michaelis's voice. He'd already been in about half an hour ago, to see how long it would be before she could finish her work. She moved away from her patient, untying the plastic apron she'd tied around her to stop splashes of plaster from attaching themselves to her uniform dress.

'Some of us don't sit behind a desk all day,' Sara said, smoothing back her unruly hair once more.

'You've just put a plaster streak on that bit of hair at the front,' Michaelis said, grinning mischievously. 'It suits you. Makes you look as if you're going prematurely white.'

'Better than highlights. Not so expensive as going to the hairdresser and plaster lasts longer,' Sara quipped. 'But I'd better remove it before it sets too hard.'

'Leave it,' Michaelis said. 'I like you with that wild, abandoned look.'

Sara could feel the unspoken promise of their night together becoming a tangible reality as they chatted together in their bantering way. From the tender expression on Michaelis's face she sensed he was feeling the same way. There was now no doubt that both of them were longing to be alone again.

'Time you went off duty, Sara.' Eleni came hurrying into the plaster room.

'Exactly what I was telling her,' Michaelis said. 'No need to stay a moment longer.'

Eleni was glancing from one to the other of them with an inquisitive expression on her face, but she didn't comment, just smiled. As the sister went out Sara could feel herself blushing.

'Give me five minutes, Michaelis,' she mumbled, and hurried away.

The harbourside was crowded with Greeks and tourists of various nationalities—English, predominantly, but also a few Germans, several French and some tall, blond Scandinavians who'd spent the day walking over the hills.

Michaelis found a vacant table by the waterside and held out a chair for Sara.

'I didn't think it would be crowded so early in the season,' she said as she sat down and looked around her.

'Just wait until August. But then, you've been here in August before. I keep forgetting all those years when you kept coming here.'

Michaelis poured her a glass of retsina and pushed a plate of olives towards her.

She bit into one of the dark bitter olives. 'You don't only forget that I've known this island a long time. Whenever I came out here you didn't seem to remember that we'd met in England either. I used to see you sometimes here in the harbourside, but you always ignored me.'

Michaelis smiled as he leaned forward and took hold of her hand. 'I recognised you, but you were always surrounded by your friends and sometimes your sisters. I didn't know whether you would have welcomed me coming forward to speak to you.'

Sara smiled. 'If you'd only known!'

'What do you mean?' Michaelis looked puzzled.

'Well…' Sara hesitated. 'I had quite a crush on you when I was a teenager.'

'A crush?'

'I thought you were terribly handsome—my kind of man, but much too old for me. And then, when you never seemed to recognise me, well…'

'And now? What do you think of me now, Sara?' Michaelis's tone was still light but there was an earnest expression on his face.

Sara took a sip from her glass before leaning back against the chair and surveying Michaelis carefully. He might look devil-may-care, this man, but he was very vulnerable. Vulnerable to her opinion of him. She would have to be very careful in what she said if she wasn't to ruin the rapport that existed between them.

'What do I think of you now?' she echoed quietly. 'I think…'

Her voice trailed away as she saw Stavros coming across from a table at the back of the taverna. His bearded face was wreathed in smiles as he arrived at their table.

'I don't wish to interrupt, but may I sit down here with you, Sara?'

'Well…' she began, but Michaelis answered for her.

'No, you may not, Stavros. Sara and I are having a quiet night out together and you haven't been invited.'

'Michaelis, I want to hear what Stavros has to say,' Sara said, and nodded at Stavros to continue.

'This will only take a moment. I telephoned your house to see when you would be home this evening, Sara, and your mother told me you would be late. I need to know if you've decided whether you can help with the music festival. Your mother tells me you received the musical score of *Ceres and Proserpine* that I sent you, and she saw you reading it, so...'

Michaelis was standing up, his tall frame menacing as he towered above the nervous Stavros.

'Don't try my patience any longer, Stavros. I insist—' He broke off and glanced around him.

The people gathered at tables inside and outside the taverna had become very quiet at the sound of Michaelis's angry voice.

Sara could see he was clenching and unclenching his hands. She felt that at any minute he might lash out and strike Stavros. And there was no comparison between the puny stature of Stavros and the tall, muscular Michaelis.

She stood up, feeling dwarfed by both men but anxious to defuse the confrontation.

'Michaelis, if you would just give me one minute to discuss the music festival with Stavros, I—'

'No, Sara!'

Michaelis looked around him again, becoming very much aware that he was causing an unwelcome tension in the taverna. If he wasn't careful all the customers would drift away to find somewhere else for the evening. His old friend, who ran this place, was coming out from behind the bar, looking extremely displeased as he wiped his hands slowly on a cloth.

Michaelis looked across at Stavros, the odious enemy who'd ruined his life. Even though he'd like to beat the hell out of the despicable little swine he had to keep his dignity. If Sara was determined to stay and talk to Stavros then there was nothing he could do. She was a free spirit, free to make her own mistakes.

Michaelis turned on his heel and walked swiftly away without a backward glance.

Sara felt a pang of anguish as she watched the retreating figure becoming enveloped in a crowd of holidaymakers.

'Stavros, I should go after Michaelis,' she said quickly.

Stavros caught hold of her arm. 'I need the help of another musician,' he said plaintively. 'You are exactly the right person for the job. I promise it won't take up too much of your time, and it would be good for you to get back into making music again.'

Watching Stavros's gentle expression, Sara felt he was right. She did need to make music again. Her medical work was satisfying, but she often longed to do something more creative in her off duty time. Somehow she would convince Michaelis that it would be OK.

'OK,' she said slowly. 'Tell me exactly what it is you're planning.'

Stavros gave Sara a beaming smile. 'You won't regret becoming involved with the festival, I promise. Sit down here for a moment, so that we can discuss what's happening.'

'Just a couple of minutes, though—I have to find Michaelis and...'

'The main project is an entirely new innovation,' Stavros said, his eyes gleaming with excitement. 'I'm planning a whole day of music in a beautiful bay down the coast from the harbour. It will be a spectacular occasion. That's when the children will perform my musical. I'd like you to help me train them, and also I need your help with the choir and the orchestra in the weeks running up to our festival in August.'

In spite of worrying about Michaelis, Sara could feel her musical interest rising. 'I do have a demanding job,' she said carefully. 'But I could spare some of my off duty time occasionally.'

'Thank you. First, I would be grateful if you could come out one day and advise me on whether you think the idea of performing my musical in a large, deserted bay is feasible. I plan to sail around to the bay next week. If you could spare the time to come with me, we could decide exactly where we would put the stage, where we would seat the orchestra, what kind of help we would need from the carpenters I've engaged and—'

'It sounds like a big project, Stavros. Are you sure...?'

'That's why I need your help, Sara. Nothing like this has ever been done on the island before. It will be spectacular!'

Sara stood up. 'I'm sure it will. If you let me know when...'

'Are you free on Sunday, Sara? My boat is still awaiting its certificate of seaworthiness, but it should be ready by then.'

Sara nodded. 'Yes, I'm off duty all day, so...'

'I'll be in touch about the arrangements then. Oh, thank you so much. Thank you, Sara!'

She said goodbye and walked away. The spectacular music project for the festival promised to be very exciting. Especially the musical. She'd read it through and was very impressed. Stavros certainly had talent.

Yes, she was glad she'd been invited to join in the musical life of the island, but what about Michaelis?

She kept on walking through the crowds, hoping to see him sitting at a table outside a taverna. She was sure he'd only marched off in a fit of pique.

Arriving at the small side street where they'd parked that evening, she was relieved to see his sturdy vehicle still standing there. No sign of Michaelis, though. Her anxiety increased.

As she started to walk back the way she'd come someone stepped out of the shadows of a doorway behind her. She turned, startled, as someone touched her shoulder.

'Oh, Michaelis! You startled me. I've been trying to find you...'

She leaned against him, sighing deeply with relief.

He drew her closer. 'I didn't want to leave until I knew you were safe.'

'Safe?' She moved in his arms and looked up at the haunted expression on his face. 'I was only having a discussion about the music festival. I know you don't like Stavros for some reason—'

'Some reason!' Michaelis held her now at arm's length, his eyes narrowing as he watched her. 'If you only knew. If—'

'Then tell me what it is you have against Stavros!' she cried, as the sheer frustration of being kept in the dark threatened to drive a wedge between them. 'Why don't you confide in me, Michaelis? So many rumours circling around and yet you refuse to take me into your confidence.'

Michaelis released her hands and took a step backwards, his face ashen beneath the sun tan. Sara watched in fear and trepidation. She'd gone too far this time. The very thing she'd planned not to do was to confront Michaelis about his secret past. How could she have been so stupid as to shatter his trust?

But she'd been tried to the limit this evening, having to contend with Michaelis walking off and leaving her like that. Now, as she watched the anguished expression on his face, she knew she should have maintained her silence. She should have remembered how she'd promised herself she wouldn't pry.

'I'll run you home now, Sara,' Michaelis said quietly, turning away and walking towards his car.

She hurried after him. 'Michaelis, I'm sorry if—'

'Leave it, Sara. That's enough for one evening.' He held open the passenger door for her. 'We both need some time alone.'

## CHAPTER NINE

IT HAD been the longest four days she'd ever known! Walking along the harbourside in the hot morning sunshine, Sara was feeling miserable. She should have been looking forward to this day out on the water, going to inspect the beautiful bay where Stavros hoped the spectacular music event would take place in August. But the deep rift between Michaelis and herself was ever present in her mind.

She glanced up at the windmills on the skyline. A heat haze was already rising up around them. She remembered how she and Michaelis had walked over there, only weeks ago. Looking back to that wonderful day, it seemed she'd been so carefree. So naïve in thinking that a wonderful romance like theirs could survive without a hitch.

She could see Stavros's boat at the end of the harbour. Perhaps when she joined in the musical life of Ceres she would be able to forget her problems. She would be able to survive without Michaelis.

Because that seemed to be where their relationship was heading. On the drive back to her house four evenings ago Michaelis had remained absolutely silent, staring ahead at the road, his fingers gripping the wheel. When they'd arrived at the house she'd tentatively asked if he would like to go inside for a drink. She hadn't been sure how her mother and sister would take this, but she hadn't cared what they thought about her relationship with Michaelis any more. She'd simply wanted to mend the rift that was opening up between Michaelis and herself. But Michaelis had shaken his head, said he needed to think, said they should take time to be alone.

She slowed her pace now, leaning against a small wall at the edge of the harbour, letting the warm sun bathe her face. It was such a perfect day for sailing on the water, though the weather forecast she'd listened to on her radio had predicted stormy conditions later in the day. Difficult to imagine when the sky was so blue. Rather like her relationship with Michaelis. One moment it had been perfect, but the next…

She took a few slow paces as she reflected that the sky had been blue every day when she'd gone into hospital since that awful evening. She'd hoped Michaelis would call her into his office, take her in his arms, tell her it was a simple lovers' tiff. But none of that had happened. He'd been cool and professional whenever they'd met in hospital. It was as if they were strangers.

She paused as she looked down into the blue waters of the harbour. A shoal of small fish was swimming past. Everything was so beautiful on this island. Everything but…

'Sara!'

She looked along the harbour and saw that Stavros had seen her. With a determined effort to function normally, she raised her hand and waved.

'Better hurry. There's a storm coming later today.'

She moved quickly now, forcing herself to think positively. She had a job to do. She would be as helpful as she could. This was an extremely worthwhile project. The children of the island would love singing and acting in Stavros's musical. The mothers and fathers would be so proud to watch them. So today she would become absorbed in the project and maybe she would begin to feel more like a human being again.

Stavros was holding out his hand towards her. She took hold of it and climbed aboard his small boat. It was one of the shabbier boats in the harbour, blue and white paint peeling off the sides, but it had passed its certificate of seaworthiness and Stavros must have proved that he was a competent sailor.

Sara forced herself to smile. '*Kalimera*, Stavros. It's difficult to believe that the weather will change today.'

Stavros glanced up at the sky. 'Oh, believe me, storms can blow up very quickly in the islands round here, so we'd better get a move on. We need to be back in harbour by mid-afternoon.'

Stavros was stepping on to the harbourside, untying the rope that was knotted around the mooring stone. Holding the rope in one hand, he prepared to get back aboard.

'Just a moment, Stavros!'

Sara felt her heart turn over as she heard Michaelis's deep, masterful, commanding voice. She'd been so intent on watching Stavros that she hadn't seen Michaelis emerging from the Sunday morning crowd who were watching the boats going out.

Wrenching the rope from Stavros's hand, Michaelis hauled the boat against the harbourside.

'What do you think you're doing, Michaelis?' Stavros said angrily. 'How dare you!'

'So it's true,' Michaelis said. 'I heard you were going out together in the boat—'

'Oh, Michaelis, please!' Sara intervened. 'We're simply going round the coast to check out the place where we want to hold part of the music festival. We'll be back this afternoon and—'

'I'm coming with you,' Michaelis said firmly.

'This is my boat—' said Stavros.

'And I'm coming with you,' Michaelis repeated, in a voice that brooked no discussion. 'I'm not going to allow Sara to be alone with you. Get in the boat, Stavros, and start the engine.'

'But—'

'Get in the boat,' Michaelis repeated with icy calm.

Gingerly, Stavros stepped aboard and moved over to start the engine. Still holding the mooring rope, Michaelis jumped from the quayside into the boat.

'Why didn't you tell me about this?' Michaelis said, looking down at Sara with anguished eyes. 'I had to hear about this from Chloe when I phoned your house this morning. Eleni told me that she'd asked if you would change your off duty today and you'd said it would be difficult as you were involved in a music project. So I phoned your house and…'

'Michaelis, we haven't been able to discuss anything together this week. Not since that evening when—'

'OK, OK!' Michaelis lowered his voice. 'But I don't want you to go out like this, alone with Stavros. I've made sure the hospital is well covered for staff today and I'll spend the day helping you.'

The noise of the engine was drowning their conversation. Stavros was looking anxiously across as he steered the boat close to the coast, but he didn't try to intervene.

Sara shook her head but decided not to say anything. She shaded her eyes with her hand, looking up at the rocky hillside that swooped down towards the sea. A goat was picking its way along the narrow waterside path, stopping occasionally to crop the sparse grass. Higher up the hill she could see a couple of tourists taking the well-defined path that would lead them over to the next bay.

Despite his behaviour, she felt glad that Michaelis was with her once again. But she was desperately apprehensive about how the three of them would get through the next few hours. There was so much tension in the air and it could only get worse.

What could have been an enjoyable day out was turning into an ordeal, and she had no idea what to do. She shivered as a cloud covered the sun, directly reflecting her own mood. Looking up, she saw several smaller clouds gathering around the sun to obscure its warmth. There was a definite swell on the surface of the water now. The wind was picking up strength, and out here on the water Sara was beginning to feel cold.

She suppressed a shiver as she wondered if Stavros was anything to do with Michaelis's secret past. For some reason or other Michaelis didn't trust Stavros. But Stavros hadn't given her any cause for concern, so she decided she would give him the benefit of the doubt.

They sailed into a large, wide, completely deserted and undeveloped bay.

'Don't you think this is a perfect setting for our project, Sara?' Stavros said, making a sweeping arc with his arms towards the approaching shore.

For a short time Sara was able to forget her misgivings and gaze around her in admiration. Even

Michaelis was looking around and nodding appreciatively.

'Yes, it should make for an exciting part of the music festival,' Michaelis said. 'But we can't stay too long today. All the signs are that the storm will arrive sooner than predicted. How long do you need to make your plans, Stavros?'

Sara felt a sense of relief that Michaelis was at last being civil towards Stavros. This was the first time he'd actually spoken to him since they'd left Ceres town.

'About three hours,' Stavros said.

Michaelis shook his head. 'No, no. Make it two, and even then we'll be pushing our luck with the weather. Come on, let's get a move on.'

He grabbed the mooring rope and leapt ashore.

'I'd like to prepare a barbecue first,' Stavros said, as he stepped ashore clutching a large wicker basket.

'No time for that,' Michaelis said firmly. 'Let's get the plans for the festival under way before we think about lunch. That's why you came, isn't it, Stavros?'

Here we go again! Sara thought, as the two men began to argue.

'Let's find the best place to position a platform for the stage where we'll perform the musical first,' Sara said, taking charge. 'Up there on the hillside would be a good place—we could have the spectators seated in an arena down here.'

'We'd better check out if a wooden platform could be erected on that rocky soil,' Michaelis said. 'The carpenters will have to know what kind of base the platform needs.'

'And we'll need to have room for the orchestra in front of the platform,' Sara said, pleased that

Michaelis appeared to be taking an interest in the project. It would help to ease the tension between him and Stavros.

There was some dissension over the siting of the platform, the open-air auditorium and the orchestra, but after a couple of hours Stavros had written down enough plans on the large notepad he'd brought with him to convince Michaelis and Sara that the festival had all the makings of a success.

Sara had become increasingly aware of the worsening weather conditions. The cold wind from the sea was strengthening and the sky was now completely overcast. The thin cotton shirt and trousers she was wearing were definitely feeling too flimsy. She was planning to put her sweater on as soon as she got back to the boat.

'I'll set up the barbecue near the boat and then we can have lunch,' Stavros said as the three of them trekked back down the hillside and walked across the shore.

'I don't think so,' Michaelis said. 'Not with clouds like that.' He swept his hand upwards towards the glowering sky. 'And look out to sea, Stavros. See the white caps on the waves? It's going to be a difficult journey even if conditions don't worsen.'

Stavros turned to look at Michaelis. 'I'd planned a civilised day out, Michaelis.'

'I'm sure you had, Stavros,' Michaelis said, placing his hands round Sara's waist and hoisting her into the boat. 'Sara, make yourself as comfortable as you can in the cabin. Stavros, go and start the engine. I'll untie the boat.'

Stavros scowled, but did as he was told. The little boat shook on the heaving waves as Michaelis leapt from the shore. Sara looked out through the salt-streaked porthole of the tiny cabin and began to feel real fear. With waves as high as this in the bay, what would it be like when they rounded the corner and hit the full strength of the wind?

She glanced at Stavros. The dark skin surrounding his beard had paled as the full realisation of this difficult voyage hit him.

'You'd better keep in the lee of the coast, Stavros,' Michaelis shouted above the noise of the engine. 'The journey from here to Ceres harbour can be tricky at the best of times. I remember one time when my father and I—'

'Shut up, Michaelis! There's no need to tell me how to sail my own boat,' Stavros retorted, opening the throttle on the engine as he began to negotiate the difficult turn around the cliffs.

Michaelis leaned over Stavros. 'If you think I'm going to—'

Michaelis's words were lost to Sara's ears as she moved swiftly out through the cabin door on to the deck. The brooding atmosphere in the cabin, coupled with the fumes from the engine, made her feel ill. How long was this dreadful journey going to take in conditions like this? The waves were buffeting against the side of the little boat. She felt really frightened as she clung to the rail.

She would take a few deep breaths and then go back into the relative safety of the cabin. The waves were enormous now. Her fingers tightened on the rail. Dared she even release her grip from the rail to take the few steps back to the cabin…?

She gave a terrified scream as a huge wave hit the side of the boat and drenched her completely. She could feel the full force of it as she tried to keep her hold on the rail. But the strength of the cascading water was dragging her over the side. Her fingers couldn't hold out against the force of the wave. She felt herself being tossed into the maelstrom of water…she was falling…she was going down…she was swallowing water…she was…

*Oh, please, please, don't let me drown! I don't want to die!*

She was kicking out with her legs, fighting with her arms to push herself back to the surface. She was a strong swimmer under normal conditions, but now her lungs felt as if they would burst. She needed air…she wanted to breathe again…she wanted this nightmare to end…

'Please, don't let me die…'

She realised that she'd actually been able to make sounds again. After her initial scream as the wave hurled her into the sea she'd been in a completely hostile environment. But strong arms were now holding her above the water. She was breathing again.

'I'm not going to die!'

'No, you're not! I've got you now, Sara.'

She could feel herself resting against Michaelis's chest in the lifesaving position as with strong, firm strokes he drew her towards the boat. Stavros had thrown a rope over the side and Sara felt herself being hoisted aboard. Michaelis clambered in after her, pulling her against him and holding her oh, so close.

He helped her into the relative warmth of the cabin. She didn't mind the smell of the fumes any more. She didn't mind anything except the fact that Michaelis had saved her life and was holding her against him as if he would never let her go.

Stavros was trying to hold a steady course near to the coastline, his hands gripping the wheel as the waves continued to buffet the little boat.

Michaelis began to strip off Sara's wet clothes, wrapping her in a blanket, cradling her against him as if she was oh, so precious to him. He paused for a few moments to drag off his own clothing, draping a blanket around his waist.

'I feel as if I've died and gone to heaven,' she murmured, as she snuggled against Michaelis's strong arms.

Looking up at him, she was alarmed to see the anguished expression on his face.

'Don't talk about dying, Sara,' he said fiercely. 'I couldn't bear to lose you. It's all so dangerously reminiscent of—'

He broke off as if momentarily realising that he mustn't continue.

'Of what, Michaelis?'

Sara could see that in Michaelis's emotionally heightened condition he was ready to talk openly at last about the secret that haunted him.

Michaelis took a deep breath. 'Reminiscent of the night my wife died.' He paused, taking more deep, rasping breaths. 'Sara, you mean everything to me. Just as my wife did until...'

Michaelis's voice petered out. His arms tightened around Sara.

'Please tell me, Michaelis.'

When at last he spoke it was as if he wasn't aware that anyone was listening.

'I was the happiest man alive when my wife told me we were going to have a baby. My life was complete. I worshipped Krisanthe. I took care of everything when she was pregnant and I longed for the birth of our child. But…'

Sara waited silently, not even stirring in Michaelis's arms for fear he would refuse to elaborate. If she could understand Michaelis's secret past perhaps he would be able to put it behind him and move on.

'When Krisanthe was about five months pregnant I had to go over to Rhodes with a patient. There was no reason to suspect what would happen that day. I'd promised to return on the evening boat, but a storm blew up and the boat was forbidden by the authorities to leave port that evening. I telephoned Krisanthe. She said she was fine. I booked into a hotel, stayed the night, and came back to Ceres in the morning, when the weather was calmer.'

Michaelis paused once more. As Sara waited for him to continue she became aware that the swell of the sea had lessened. The boat wasn't rocking so violently any more. The storm was blowing over them, transferring to some other island in these stormy seas. It must have been like that when Michaelis had wanted to get back to his pregnant wife. And then had come the calm of the day after. But what had Michaelis found on his return?

She glanced at Stavros, aware that because the storm had receded he could now hear what was being said. He was looking decidedly distraught.

'So, you came back to Ceres, Michaelis?' Sara prompted. 'And…?'

'I unlocked the door. It seemed strange that Krisanthe had decided to lock it. We never lock doors on Ceres. But then I remembered that it was normal if she was alone.' Michaelis drew in his breath. 'I found her lying on the bathroom floor covered in blood.'

Sara gasped at the horrific revelation. 'But—'

'I cradled her in my arms. At first she was completely motionless, but as I moved her she opened her eyes. I said I was going to take her to hospital but she begged me not to. She said she knew she was going to die. And then came the awful revelation... She said she didn't want to live. She didn't deserve to live. Now that she knew she was dying she wanted to confess everything...'

Sara strained her ears to hear what Michaelis was saying. Had she misheard him?

'To confess everything?' she repeated softly.

Michaelis nodded.

'I said that whatever she had to say I was taking her to the hospital. But she tried to shake me off. She told me it was too late. She'd wanted to die ever since she found out she was pregnant. She said that when she'd started to miscarry during the night she'd known it was a judgement, a punishment.'

'But what had Krisanthe—?'

'She showed me the tiny, dead foetus wrapped in a towel. She begged me to leave her to die. Not to take her to the hospital. She said she was slipping peacefully away. No pain...'

'But why? Why did she do it?' Sara said.

'Because the child wasn't mine. She told me—'

'No!' Stavros's anguished voice filled the cabin.

'Yes,' Michaelis said icily. 'Krisanthe told me about the night she'd spent with you, Stavros. It was during the month I was in England. She knew it wasn't my baby right from the start.'

Stavros bent his head over the wheel. 'I didn't

know I'd made Krisanthe pregnant, Michaelis. She never spoke to me again. We were both so ashamed after it happened. Let me explain. I—'

'Be quiet, Stavros!' Michaelis thundered. 'As Krisanthe lay dying in my arms she begged me not to confront you. She knew her secret would come out if I sought you out and beat the hell out of you…which is what I've wanted to do every day since she told me. I promised I wouldn't, and I also promised not to tell her family. Keeping those two promises has been the hardest thing I've ever had to do, but it was a question of honour. I vowed never to compromise my honour, nor that of Krisanthe's family. I'm not proud of breaking my silence now, but in the heat of the moment, holding Sara in my arms, fearing she might die in the water, it brought it all back to me…'

'I feel honoured that you've told me,' Sara said gently. 'I've wanted to know what was troubling you. I've wanted to share your grief. We can move on now.'

'I hope so!' He held her closer in his arms. 'It was just like this, the night Krisanthe died. As soon as she'd finished her confession she closed her eyes. I could see she was slipping away, but I hoped there was a chance I could save her. I lifted her in my arms and carried her out through the streets of the village to where I'd parked my car. Several people saw me carrying Krisanthe, saw the blood on the blanket, saw her body in my arms… But I've never discussed it with anybody. How could I when I was sworn to silence? And all because…'

Slowly Michaelis released Sara from his arms and

stood up, advancing menacingly towards Stavros. The boat had ceased to rock; the waves had calmed.

Sara hauled herself to her feet, clutching the blanket around her like a giant shawl.

'Don't, Michaelis!' she cried, putting out her hand pleadingly. 'I know Stavros ruined your life, but—'

'Let me explain,' Stavros shouted, holding his arms in front of his face as if to fend off a blow.

Michaelis lunged forward. For a second Sara thought he was going to hit Stavros, but he was merely grabbing the wheel, which was spinning out of control now that Stavros was so distraught.

Stavros sank to the floor and took his head in his hands. Between sobs he tried to explain.

'I never meant it to happen, Michaelis.'

Stony-faced, Michaelis steered the boat, looking straight ahead of him.

'It was just the once. On the night it happened Krisanthe had been to my choir practice. She had a good voice, if you remember, and—'

'Stick to the point, Stavros,' Michaelis said in an ominous tone.

'Krisanthe seemed so lonely while you were in England. I asked if she'd like me to walk her home. As we passed my house I invited her in for a drink.'

'Krisanthe didn't drink—not alcohol, Stavros.'

'She told me she was missing you terribly, Michaelis, and she found difficulty sleeping. I said a Metaxa brandy would help her sleep.'

'So you plied her with drink,' Michaelis said scornfully.

'No! I simply gave her a glass of Metaxa. She said she enjoyed it and asked for another one. We...we both drank too much after that, and one thing led to another…'

'Michaelis, you promised Krisanthe to keep her secret,' Sara said quickly as Michaelis moved towards Stavros. 'You've kept your promise all these years. Now Stavros knows the truth he'll have to keep it a secret too.'

'You're right, Sara,' Michaelis said slowly, his fingers clenching and unclenching. He turned to look at the terrified Stavros. 'You're lucky I don't beat you to a pulp. But if you speak one word to Krisanthe's parents, I'll knock the hell out of you until—'

'I promise, Michaelis! I give you my word. This awful secret will go with me to the grave. I'm so ashamed. I'm so…'

'OK, just get this boat safely into the harbour and we'll never speak about it again.' Michaelis held out his hand towards Stavros. 'I can keep a promise. I hope you can.'

Stavros took one hand off the wheel and held it out towards Michaelis.

Sara gave a sigh of relief as she watched the two men shaking hands.

There were crowds of people, mostly tourists, lining the harbourside as Stavros and Michaelis moored the boat. Rummaging in the wooden lockers under the seats in the cabin, Michaelis had found some oilskin trousers and jacket for himself and a pair of old jeans and a sweater which completely swamped Sara.

Sara glanced down at her strange clothes as she prepared to make her way through the crowd of Sunday evening revellers.

'We were so worried about you, Michaelis,' one

Greek man called out as he watched Michaelis tying up the boat. 'Soon after you'd set off the police put out a message over the radio for all boats to return to port. Didn't you hear it?'

'Stavros's radio is on the blink,' Sara said, taking hold of Michaelis's hand as she stepped ashore.

An Englishwoman touched her arm. 'Whatever happened to you, dear? You look as if you nearly drowned. There were ever so many people praying for your safe return when we went into the church.'

'That was kind of them,' Sara said, and she leaned against Michaelis, feeling suddenly exhausted.

Michaelis put his arm around her and held her close against his side. 'I'll get you back to the car.'

'Sara? Sara!'

Chloe was pushing her way through the crowd to reach the harbourside. 'We've been so worried about you. Are you all right?'

'I'm fine!' Sara's voice wavered as she felt herself going faint.

'I've just come off duty. I've got Dad's car up at the hospital. I'll drive you back home.'

'I'm going to take Sara back to my house,' Michaelis said firmly.

He smiled down at Sara and she felt a warm glow of love flowing through her entire body. Michaelis had recovered from the anguish of his revelation. He looked strong, calm and confident again, as if sharing his awful secret with her had given him his life back.

'With respect, Michaelis,' Chloe said, 'I think Sara needs to return home, where she can recover from her ordeal. Don't you Sara?'

Sara looked from one to the other of them. Sisterly love was one thing. But at a time like this she needed strong, loving arms around her. The decision was easy.

'I'm going with Michaelis,' she said quietly. 'I'll see you tomorrow.'

Chloe leaned forward and gave Sara a kiss on the cheek. 'I hope you know what you're doing, Sara,' she whispered.

'Oh, I certainly do,' Sara whispered back, just before her legs gave way beneath her.

As she crumpled to the floor she felt Michaelis taking control again. With a swift swoop towards her he scooped her up into his arms and carried her away. The crowd parted as the strangely dressed yet devastatingly handsome man took charge of his exhausted girlfriend.

'I feel as if I'm floating on air,' Sara said, trying desperately to gather her strength as she clung to Michaelis.

He looked down at her. 'You need a thorough medical check by a first-class doctor.'

He was lifting her inside the car now. She slumped back against the seat and gave a sigh.

'So, where could we find a first-class doctor on a Sunday on a remote Greek island?' she asked, enjoying the feeling of total irresponsibility.

Michaelis feigned solemnity as he started the engine. 'Difficult question, but I think I know just the man. Not cheap, but you might be able to repay him somehow. Shall we go up to his house? He has this strange house…'

'Is it halfway up a hill, in the middle of nowhere?'

'Exactly! You sound as if you've been there before.'

'Oh, I know it well…but not well enough,' Sara

whispered, as she snuggled against Michaelis. 'I spent such a wonderful night there, long, long ago—at least, it seems like long ago now, but actually…'

Her eyelids were oh, so heavy. She didn't want to miss a moment of her time with Michaelis, so she would just close them for a second…

# CHAPTER TEN

SARA opened her eyes and looked around her. The sky outside the windows was dark. Where was she? A light was burning on the bedside table beside her. She was in a large bed, all by herself…

It was as if a dense fog was clouding over her thoughts, making it impossible to… Yes, it was Michaelis's bed. But where was Michaelis and what…?

'You're awake!' Michaelis came striding into the room, the anxious expression on his face changing to one of deep tenderness as he sat down on the bed beside her.

Sara noticed he was fully clothed in jeans and sweatshirt, even though it was obviously the middle of the night.

'What happened? I don't remember coming up to bed.'

'You were asleep when I carried you in from the car. I think the events of the day were all too much for you. I brought you straight up here and put you to bed.' He gave her a wry smile. 'I hope you approve of the nightshirt you're wearing. It was all I could find and you had a low temperature. I was tempted to warm you with my body, but decided you needed to sleep.'

Sara stirred languidly. Her body felt warm now as she curled inside Michaelis's huge cotton shirt. There was a faint scent of his aftershave still lingering around the collar, and that strange, indefinably masculine aroma that was already heightening her senses.

'I still feel cold, Michaelis,' she said, in her most seductive voice, and she held back the sheet.

Michaelis put out a hand and covered her forehead. 'You feel pretty hot to me. Perhaps I should take your temperature again.'

'Later, Michaelis,' she whispered, her voice betraying the passionate hunger she was feeling.

All trace of her exhaustion had left her as she reached out to touch him. Swiftly, he shrugged out of his clothes. The sight of Michaelis's hard, virile body sent shivers of delicious anticipation down her spine.

'Yes, oh, yes,' she whispered as he climbed in beside her, taking her in his arms, his strong firm fingers caressing her and causing liquid fire to ignite in every part of her body.

She was in heaven again. She'd always hoped to recreate the idyllic moments they'd spent together last time they were here in this bed, and now, as Michaelis coaxed every atom of her being into warm, sensual arousal, she moaned with ecstasy, urging him to go on but at the same time longing for the ultimate climactic release. When it happened she cried out and clung to Michaelis, wanting to hold him inside her till the end of time…

The phone was ringing. Sara opened her eyes. The faint light of dawn was creeping over the windowsill. Michaelis released her from their sleeping embrace and reached for the phone.

'Yes, this is Dr Michaelis Stangos. I was expecting your call, but not quite so soon…. It's all arranged?

Thank you. I'll bring the patients over this morning, as you suggest… Yes, of course I will.'

He put down the phone and turned to look at Sara, his face wreathed in smiles. 'We've done it! Rhodes Hospital has agreed to take them today.'

'Who?' Sara sat up, pushing back the hair from her eyes.

'Our kidney patients… Oh, sorry, Sara—I'd forgotten you were asleep when I answered the phone last night. Ariadne's mother arrived on the island yesterday. She flew in to Athens and took the overnight ferry, landing in Ceres during the morning. She went straight to the hospital.'

'But why hadn't she told us she was arriving?'

Michaelis smiled. 'As you probably gathered when you spoke to her on the phone, Sylvia Greenwood is a creature of impulse. As soon as she got the results of the tests from the Australian hospital and found she was compatible with her daughter in tissue type she got her mother-in-law to take charge of her family and then went straight to the airport and got on the first plane.'

'Where is she now?'

'Eleni gave her a bed in a private room for the night. She was tired and jet lagged and it didn't seem a good idea to have a reunion between mother and daughter at that point. Late last night Eleni phoned me and told me what had happened. I agreed to take over the case from there.'

'And it sounds as if you've already been in touch with Rhodes.'

Michaelis nodded. 'I didn't want to waste any time. There's one particular surgeon who's excellent at kidney transplants. I wanted to make sure he would take over the case from me. He's just agreed now. He was particularly keen on the case history I gave him last night. He'll start more tests and prepare both mother and daughter during the coming week before operating as soon as it can be arranged.'

'But that's wonderful! And Ariadne knows nothing about this yet?'

Michaelis shook his head. 'Eleni thought that as you and I had dealt with Ariadne's case from the start we should be the ones to give her the good news.'

'And introduce her to her mother,' Sara said quietly.

'Exactly! I'm not sure how that will go... Nobody can predict how mother and daughter will react. But I'm sure that Ariadne's gratitude will help her to get over the awful knowledge that she was abandoned as a baby.'

'And I'm sure when Sylvia explains all the circumstances Ariadne will get rid of her resentment,' Sara said.

'I hope so. But we'll both have to be there to ensure the reunion is a success. And then we have to persuade both of them to come with us to the hospital today.'

'You want me to go over to Rhodes with you, Michaelis?'

He looked surprised at her question. 'Of course. You're the main part of my team. I can't do this without you. That is, unless you're feeling too tired?'

She smiled. 'Are you referring to my near drowning yesterday, or...?'

He leaned forward and took her in his arms. 'You're a remarkable girl, Sara. A wonderful, brilliant, fantastic girl. I thought I'd lost you yesterday, but you came back to me, and now I'm going to make sure I never lose you again. Sara…oh, Sara…'

He paused, looking down into her eyes with the most tender expression. 'I want to say this in English, so forgive me if it doesn't come out right. Sara, will you marry me? Will you be my wife? Will you stay with me for ever and—?'

'Yes, yes, yes—I will.'

He drew her closer, his lips seeking hers once more. 'We have to be at the hospital in an hour. Not much time, but…'

This time their coming together was tender, exquisite, the lovemaking of a couple who knew they had the rest of their lives to spend with each other…

It was mid-morning when the air ambulance flew over the sparkling blue sea. Sara looked down at the tiny boats beneath them.

'A different day from yesterday, Michaelis,' she said quietly.

'Yes, in more ways than one.'

He reached across and took hold of her hand. It was a most unprofessional action, especially as she was in uniform and they were both on duty. But their patients didn't need any medical treatment at the moment.

Looking across at mother and daughter now, Sara felt a warm, happy feeling at a job well done. Their part of the work would soon be over, when they delivered their patients to the hospital. They would take over the post-operative care when the patients were transferred back to Ceres, but for the moment there was nothing more they could do.

Sara remembered the mother and daughter reunion

earlier this morning. She needn't have been apprehensive. As she had hoped, Sylvia had won over her daughter almost immediately. Sylvia was now talking quietly to Ariadne. From snippets of the conversation Sara gathered that she was filling in the details of her life since she'd had to leave Ariadne behind on Ceres.

'My heart was broken, darling,' Sara heard Sylvia saying. 'You were such a beautiful baby, Ariadne, you were my pride and joy. I'd planned to take you with me to Australia, but…'

'I know—I know, Mum. I understand. I just wish I'd known you all those years when I was growing up.'

Sylvia put an arm around her daughter's shoulders and hugged her. 'We'll have to make up for lost time now, my love.'

Michaelis leaned forward. 'You'll have plenty of time together during the next few days before the operation. You'll be able to really get to know each other in the hospital.'

'Oh, we know each other well enough now,' Ariadne said. 'I feel as if Mum's never been away.'

'Thanks for everything you two have done for us,' Sylvia said. She hesitated. 'Do I gather that congratulations are in order?'

Michaelis gave a wry smile. 'What makes you think that, Sylvia?'

'Well, the way you two keep looking at each other, for a start. You've got to be the happiest couple I've seen in a long time.'

'Well, you're the first to know,' Michaelis said, his smile broadening as he gave up trying to disguise his feelings for Sara. 'Earlier this morning I asked Sara to marry me…and she said yes.'

'Well, of course she said yes! By the look on her pretty face… Congratulations, both of you!' Sylvia said. 'I hope you'll be as happy as Don and me have been.'

'I'm sure we will,' Michaelis said, bringing Sara's hand to his lips. 'I'm the luckiest man in the world.'

'When we come back to Ceres, will you still be able to look after us, Doctor?' Ariadne asked. 'I mean, you're not planning to fly off on honeymoon are you?'

Michaelis laughed. 'We haven't made any plans at all. Haven't had time. I still have to go round and ask Sara's father's permission. It's tradition!'

For a moment Sara felt a pang of apprehension despite her smile. There had been an undercurrent of mistrust concerning Michaelis in her family recently. She hoped that she could convince Chloe and her mother that marrying Michaelis was going to make her the happiest girl in the world. She was going to do it anyway, but having the whole family's blessing would mean a lot to her.

The helicopter touched down on the Ceres landing pad. After they'd settled their patients in hospital they'd made a speedy return.

Michaelis had left his car nearby and Sara leaned back against the passenger seat as he drove along the coastal road towards Nymborio.

'Ariadne and Sylvia were getting on well when we left them, weren't they?' She smiled. 'I'm glad you know the surgeon. Such a nice man!'

'Oh, Patris will keep us informed every step of the way. We trained in surgery together at an Athens hospital. He went on to become a top surgeon. I stayed on the sidelines as a multi-purpose small island doctor.'

Sara snuggled up to him. 'I'm glad you did. Otherwise we might never have got to know each other.'

'It was destiny we should meet,' Michaelis said huskily. 'You've made such a difference to my life, Sara. Will you come with me to see my parents when we've seen yours? I know they'll be thrilled when I tell them the good news. They were both so happy to meet you, and yet I kept them in the dark about how things were going between us.'

'There was a time, not so long ago, when neither of us knew how things were going between us,' Sara said quietly. 'Of course I'll go with you to tell your parents the good news.'

They were nearing the house in Nymborio now. Sara tried not to show that she was feeling nervous.

Michaelis cut the engine, opened the passenger door and helped Sara down on to the stony parking area in front of the house. The lights were on in the upstairs sitting room. Chloe came out on to the balcony at the sound of the engines and waved when she saw her sister.

Michaelis held on to Sara's hand as they climbed the short path that led to the house. Together they walked up the steps to the sitting room. The door was open. Chloe came to meet them. She kissed her sister on the cheek before holding out her hand to Michaelis.

'Welcome, Michaelis,' she said, in a formal, polite voice.

'Come in—come in, Michaelis!' Anthony Metcalfe

had been out in the garden at the back of the house and now followed them up the stairs.

Sara felt a sense of relief. Of all the members in her family her father had never been a party to listening to island tittle-tattle. He'd always liked Michaelis, from the time when he'd been one of his students for that month-long course in England. And Sara had noticed that her mother and sister never dared to voice their doubts about Michaelis's integrity in front of Anthony.

'We haven't seen anything of you for weeks.' Anthony was pumping Michaelis's hand. 'I suggested to Pam that you should join us at Easter for some of our celebrations, but she said she thought you would be on duty—being the medical director and so on. It must be a tough job at times. I know what it's like. Responsibility! I'd rather go fishing.'

'Sir, I've come to ask you something,' Michaelis said, in a firm voice that belied the apprehension he felt. 'I've known for some time that there are certain rumours going around about me…'

Sara glanced at her mother and sister, who appeared to be studying the design on the carpet in front of their feet.

'Rumours?' Anthony looked genuinely surprised. 'I never listen to rumour. What are the rumours about?'

'My first wife died in tragic circumstances, miscarrying a son. It was totally unexpected and I wasn't able to be there until it was too late to save her life. Certain people pointed the finger at me and deduced that I was an uncaring husband…or even worse that I was in some way…'

'Michaelis, please—if I may say something?' Sara said quietly. 'Michaelis's wife disclosed a tragic secret just before she died, and she made him promise never to reveal it to anyone. Because Michaelis is an honourable man he has kept his promise to remain silent. And this is why rumours have built up. I can assure you that they are completely unfounded. I love Michaelis very much, and—'

'Sara, I'd like to ask your father first, before you say anything more.' Michaelis turned to Anthony. 'I would like to ask for your daughter's hand in marriage, sir.'

Sara felt a lump rising in her throat. Hearing the quaint old-fashioned phrase spoken in Michaelis's charmingly accented voice brought tears to her eyes. Her mother had risen to her feet and now hurried over to put her arms around Sara.

Chloe joined in the hugging of her sister. 'I'm sorry, Sara,' she whispered. 'I never really doubted. Mum and I just wanted to make sure you would be happy. You're so precious to all of us.'

'Of course you have my blessing, Michaelis,' Anthony said delightedly.

He turned to look at his daughter. 'I hope you've already accepted, Sara?'

Sara dried her eyes on the tissue her mother was holding out towards her. 'Of course I have!'

'This calls for champagne!' Anthony said. 'Chloe, go and find Manolis. Ask him to bring one of the magnums from the cellar. The good stuff I open on special occasions—not that fizzy cheap rubbish you girls keep buying.'

The moon was high in the sky by the time Michaelis and Sara got back to the house on the hill. A lone goat on the hillside began bleating as they climbed out of the car.

'Phew! Talk about a whistlestop tour of the parents!' Sara said, leaning for a moment against Michaelis as he set her down on the ground.

He drew her against him. 'You made my parents so happy just now. My mother had begun to doubt I would ever get over my first wife. She nagged and pried but I couldn't open up to her. But now I'm going to have a new wife she knows that what happened all those years ago doesn't matter any more. It's all in the past. Do you know what she's looking forward to now?'

Sara smiled as she looked up at the moon. The man in the moon seemed to be winking at her. She knew what most mothers wanted when a son was about to get married.

'I couldn't possibly guess,' she said lightly.

'Mother told me she's longing for us to start a family. The sooner the better, she said. I thought maybe we could make a start tonight.'

Sara could feel warm desire for the love of her life running through her again. Tonight would be special. Tonight they'd resolved all their problems.

'I think that would be a perfect idea,' she said softly, as Michaelis scooped her up in his arms and carried her over the threshold of her new home.

# Don't miss *Book Seven* of this BRAND-NEW 12 book collection 'Bachelor Auction'.

Who says money can't buy love?

## *On sale 7th March*

*Available at most branches of WH Smith, Tesco, Martins, Borders, Eason, Sainsbury's, and all good paperback bookshops.*

BA/RTL/7

## Become a Panel Member

If YOU are a regular United Kingdom buyer of Mills & Boon® Medical Romance™ you might like to tell us your opinion of the books we publish to help us in publishing the books *you* like.
Mills & Boon have a Reader Panel of Medical Romance™ readers. Each person on the panel receives a short questionnaire (taking about five minutes to complete) every third month asking for opinions of the past month's Medical Romances. All people who send in their replies have a chance of winning a FREE year's supply of Medical Romances.
If YOU would like to be considered for inclusion on the panel please fill in and return the following survey. We can't guarantee that everyone will be on the panel but first come will be first considered.

Where did you buy this novel?

❑ WH Smith
❑ Tesco
❑ Borders
❑ Sainsbury's
❑ Direct by mail
❑ Other (please state) ________________________________

What themes do you enjoy most in the Mills & Boon® novels that you read? (Choose all that apply.)

❑ Amnesia
❑ Family drama (including babies/young children)
❑ Hidden/Mistaken identity
❑ Historical setting
❑ Marriage of convenience
❑ Medical drama
❑ Mediterranean men
❑ Millionaire heroes
❑ Mock engagement or marriage
❑ Outback setting
❑ Revenge

- ❑ Sheikh heroes
- ❑ Secret baby
- ❑ Shared pasts
- ❑ Western

On average, how many Mills & Boon® novels do you read every month? ____________

Please provide us with your name and address:

Name: ____________________________
Address: ____________________________
____________________________
____________________________
____________________________

What is your occupation?
(OPTIONAL)
____________________________

In which of the following age groups do you belong?
(OPTIONAL)

- ❑ 18 to 24
- ❑ 25 to 34
- ❑ 35 to 49
- ❑ 50 to 64
- ❑ 65 or older

**Thank you for your help!**
**Your feedback is important in helping us offer quality products you value.**

**The Reader Service**
**Reader Panel Questionnaire**
**FREEPOST CN81**
**Croydon CR9 3WZ**

MEDRD502

MEDICAL SURVEY B